"A month," Kelly said.

"With a partner," she added as clarification since Durant wasn't answering her. Not if that disinterested look he'd just sent her way was any indication. "Is that the life expectancy of a partnership with you?"

Kane shrugged, apparently totally uninterested in her choice of topics to verbally pursue. "Give or take," he finally replied vaguely, aware of the way she was looking at him, waiting for an answer. "I don't keep track."

Or so he thought.

Kelly nodded. "Fair enough," she told him. "I just wanted to know what I was up against, that's all."

"What's *that* supposed to mean?" Kane asked.

"I'm going to look at this partnership as a challenge. If I can hang on beyond a certain point, say longer than your longest lasting partner, then it's okay. I made it. You know, kind of like staying on a bucking horse for eight seconds."

He looked at her as if she were a few cards short of a complete deck. If the woman wanted a challenge, he had one for her.

***

Be sure to check out the next books in

Cavanagh Justice—
Where Aurora's finest are always in action

HOW TO SEDUCE
A CAVANAUGH

BY
MARIE FERRARELLA

Published in Great Britain 2015
by Mills & Boon, an imprint of Harlequin (UK) Limited,
Eton House, 18-24 Paradise Road, Richmond, Surrey, TW9 1SR

© 2015 Marie Rydzynski-Ferrarella

ISBN: 978-0-263-91544-0

18-0715

Harlequin (UK) Limited's policy is to use papers that are natural, renewable and recyclable products and made from wood grown in sustainable forests. The logging and manufacturing processes conform to the legal environmental regulations of the country of origin.

Printed and bound in Spain
by CPI, Barcelona

USA TODAY bestselling and RITA® Award-winning author **Marie Ferrarella** has written more than two hundred and fifty books for Mills & Boon, some under the name Marie Nicole. Her romances are beloved by fans worldwide. Visit her website, www.marieferrarella. com.

To anyone who has ever read anything I've ever written, thank you! Without you, the fantasies wouldn't come true.

Prologue

Fear clawed at his small, heaving chest. It felt like long, sharp nails tearing into his very flesh.

He was aware of breathing hard, of being dizzy because he was unable to get in enough air.

A feeling of déjà vu oppressively weighed him down, pressing harder than an actual boulder could.

He'd been through this before, felt this way before, even though it was happening right before his eyes, so achingly vivid he couldn't look away.

Not even for an instant.

Not even if his own survival depended on it.

Kane Durant was small for his age. But even if he hadn't been, if he had been bigger and stronger than he actually was, he still would have been powerless against the big man.

Powerless to make him stop.

His father was a hulk of a man and only seemed to become more so when he was enraged.

Just the way he was now.

Enraged and spewing obscenities, hurling them at the trembling woman kneeling before him on the cracked vinyl kitchen floor.

The bruises on his mother's face from his father's last eruption were just now beginning to fade. The arguments, the rages, they were occurring more and more frequently these days, leaving an ugly rainbow of colors on every limb of her body.

The sense of constant anxiety never really went away anymore.

From the very moment he opened his eyes in the morning, Kane felt the frightening tension. Even during the lulls, which came less and less frequently, he knew it was just a matter of time before the next vicious outburst happened.

He'd been in his bed, fearfully watching the shadows moving on his ceiling when he'd heard his father bellowing, heard his mother crying out in fear and then in pain.

He was just a scrawny boy of ten, but the moment he heard his father yelling at his mother, he had abandoned his room and run into the kitchen to try to help his mother in any way he could.

To protect her.

Thin and fragile, she was no match against his father's wrath.

Neither was he, but maybe together…

Kane had gotten to the kitchen just as his father's anger had hit a new high.

The flash from the handgun seized his attention as he struggled to process what he saw. What his brain already knew. He was terrified.

He ran to his mother to block the bullet, to divert it from its course.

But he was too late.

The bullet from his father's handgun had found its intended target less than a split second earlier.

His mother's face abruptly froze, highlighting surprise and pain. And then she pitched backward. Blood poured freely from the newly created hole in her abdomen.

Kane opened his mouth to scream his protest, but nothing came out. Not a single sound came out to express his fear, his anger, his horrified outrage at the senselessness of it all.

Unable to voice his reaction, Kane put all his energy into attempting to stop the bleeding. But his hands were too small for the task. Blood squeezed its way through his delicate, ineffective fingers, underscoring his helplessness.

"Don't die. Don't leave me. Please don't leave me," he begged the woman who was already gone.

His voice only served to irritate his father further. "You love her that much, you little bastard? Then you're going to join her!"

The next second he heard his father's gun discharge. Felt something sharp and painful tear through his chest. Felt something else oozing out.

Blood.

Was that his?

Yes. He was bleeding. His blood was mingling with his mother's.

He sank to his knees in slow motion.

At least it felt that way. The last thing he heard was the roar of the handgun again.

The last thing he saw was his father going down.

A cry of traumatized anguish tore from his lips. The sound of heavy breathing echoed in the empty room as he bolted upright.

In his bed.

In his bedroom.

Kane looked down at his torso, checking for bullet holes. There were none. Just the scar of one, but it had healed.

He was soaked, but it was with sweat, not blood.

Shaking, Kane dragged his hand through his hair, doing his best to reclaim some sort of calm, and then resigning himself to the fact that he wasn't going to find it in what was left of the night.

The dream had found him again.

He hadn't had it in a long, long time, but now it

was back, forcing him back to square one. He had to work at getting himself back on an even keel.

Again.

He was exhausted—and restless beyond words.

Throwing off the covers, he got up. Beyond his window, darkness still embraced the city of Aurora, but there was no way he was going to go back to sleep. Not now.

Resigned, Kane made his way to the kitchen, fervently wishing he hadn't given up smoking last month.

It looked as if his nerves were going to have to calm down on their own.

He bit off a couple of colorful words under his breath.

It wasn't going to be easy.

Chapter 1

The detective was ignoring her.

Well, not so much *ignoring* her, Kelly Cavanaugh silently amended, as acting as if no one else was sitting in the chief of detectives' office, waiting for the man to come in, except for him.

They actually did know one another—by sight at least—from the department they both worked in. Robbery, a division in the Aurora Police Department, wasn't huge, but it wasn't exactly miniscule, either. She saw Detective Kane Durant in passing almost every day. He'd even nodded at her a couple of times in response to her voiced greeting, but they had never had any sort of conversation—not even an inane one—and that was on him. Kane Durant apparently wasn't one for small talk.

He didn't seem to be one for big talk, either, Kelly thought now, even though she had tried to draw him out a time or two. His responses involved the absolute minimum of words. If something called for five words, she would offer ten if not more. Durant, however, seemed to be the type who would be hard-pressed to render more than three under the same set of circumstances.

Doing her best not to fidget, Kelly tried engaging the stoic, dark blond detective in some sort of conversation now. The reason for that was her curiosity had gotten the best of her.

"Do you know why we're here?"

Durant continued staring straight ahead, as if he was memorizing the titles of the books on the shelf behind the chief's desk.

Just when she decided he was going to continue ignoring her, the detective answered in a monotone voice, "Chief of ds called us in."

She took a breath. "Fair enough." If the man had been any stiffer he easily could have played the part of the Tin Man in a production of *The Wizard of Oz*. Willing to give the stoic detective the benefit of the doubt, she told herself that maybe she should have been more specific in her query. "Do you know *why* he called us in?"

"No." The answer was given to the bookshelf, not to her.

Kelly shook her head. She'd heard of the strong, silent type, but this was carrying things a bit too far. "You know, I had a hand puppet as a kid that talked more than you do."

This time, Kane spared her a glance before turning back around. It wasn't exactly the kind of look that warmed a person's soul, Kelly noted. It was meant to cut someone dead.

Lucky for her, she had a thick skin and didn't take offense easily.

Just then she heard the door behind them open.

Thank God! Kelly thought.

It was all she could do to keep from breathing a huge sigh of relief. The ordeal of sitting here with this exceptionally good-looking sphinx hopefully would be over with soon.

To acknowledge the chief's presence, both she and the silent detective rose from their seats.

"Sorry to keep you two waiting. I'm afraid I'm running a little behind today. But I didn't have Raleigh bring you here to listen to my excuses."

Rounding his desk, Brian Cavanaugh, Aurora PD's chief of detectives as well as Kelly's granduncle, greeted both detectives in his office with an easy smile.

"Sit, please," he told the duo, underscoring his

words with a hand gesture that indicated they should sink back into the seats they had vacated.

Like everyone else in his family, Brian Cavanaugh had worked his way up in the ranks. He'd held down his current position for a number of years now and, by all accounts, the men and women who served under him gave him not only their undying loyalty but their admiration, as well. That, to him, was far better than any badge of honor or official recognition he would ever receive.

His intent was to always do right by the department's men and women.

"Do either of you know why I called you in?" Brian asked, looking from the solemn-faced detective to his far more cheerful grandniece.

He was looking at two completely different people. One reminded him of a sunny spring morning; the other made him think of a pending storm rolling in in the middle of the night.

Neither, however, was answering the question he had posed.

This was Brian's first official meeting with Durant and, actually, his first professional meeting with Kelly, as well. The handful of other times he had interacted with the young woman had all taken place at his older brother's house. Andrew Cavanaugh, the former police chief, was wont to use absolutely any available excuse to get their extended clan together to break bread and just unwind.

Brian regarded the two detectives for a moment before assuring them genially, "There're no points taken off for a wrong answer."

Kelly slanted a quick glance at the man to her right. His was a profile that lent itself well to one of those Greek statues she'd seen on the museum field trips her mother had insisted on years ago.

Durant probably had the warmth of one of those statues as well, she couldn't help thinking. She tried to recall if she had ever seen the man smile when their paths had crossed.

She couldn't remember a single instance.

Since the stoic detective wasn't saying anything, she decided to go first. "Well, I don't know about Detective Durant, but I'm thinking that you called me in because of Amos."

Even saying the man's name brought in a wave of sadness to her.

Detective Amos Barkley was her partner. Or rather, he had been until last week. After twenty-one years on the job, her friend and mentor had put in his papers. He'd said he'd protected and served long enough, and now he wanted to do something for himself. Informing her before he made his intentions public, Amos had told her that he wanted to go fishing "before I'm just too damn old to hold on to a fishing pole and land anything bigger than a minnow."

Those also had been his words, addressed to people in the squad room, during the retirement party she had thrown for him at the station. It had made her wonder if Amos had been trying to convince his friends or himself as to his reasons for retiring.

Kane, she'd noted at the time, had been the only one who hadn't officially attended Amos's retirement party. He'd been in squad room during the celebration, but he had employed what she could only think of as tunnel vision, managing to block out everything that had been going on except for the paperwork he'd been focusing on.

He'd even turned down a slice of the three-layer cake she'd had brought in from Amos's favorite bakery. Detectives from several other departments had turned up for the going-away party, but Durant had deliberately isolated himself from it and then promptly disappeared at the very height of the celebration.

Brian nodded at her response. "Yes, I did," he confirmed. "That's also, in part, why I called you in as well, Durant," he said, this time directing his words to the solemn detective. "Captain Collins," he went on, citing the head of the robbery division, "told me that your current partner requested to either have a new partner assigned to him or to be transferred out of Robbery and into another division entirely. According to him, he didn't care which it was, as long as it didn't involve you."

Brian paused as if he was waiting for his words to sink in.

"How many partners does that make, detective?" he asked the younger man.

"Three," Kane replied in a voice that gave no indication if it bothered him in the slightest that his partners all had sought to get away from him.

"Since you were assigned to Robbery," Brian agreed, nodding his head. "And how many partners before that?"

"Two," Kane replied, again without hesitation.

"Three," Brian corrected.

"Technically, Rawlins didn't request a transfer," Kane said, his voice devoid of emotion. "He was shot and decided he wanted to pursue a different career." It was highly likely that had that not happened, the man would have requested a transfer, but Kane assumed the chief was dealing in facts, not conjecture.

Brian inclined his head as if willing to go with the younger man's version of the circumstances.

"I'll accept that," Brian allowed. And then he got down to the heart of the meeting he had called. "You're a good, reliable detective who is outstanding at his job," he acknowledged. "At the same time, unfortunately, getting along with people doesn't exactly seem to be your strong suit, Detective Durant."

Kane didn't waste his breath by denying the chief's observation. There was no point, especially since what the chief said was essentially true.

"I do better on my own, sir," Kane replied quietly.

"You may think that," Brian allowed. "But no one

does better alone." He said the words like a man who was firmly convinced in his stand. He left no room for either argument or speculation. "You need a partner to pick up on things you might have missed, to watch your back and," he continued, looking at Kane pointedly, "to keep you grounded."

The last thing he needed was someone *grounding* him. To Kane that was just another way of saying "interfering." He didn't like being interfered with.

"With all due respect, sir, I don't need someone yapping at my heels, telling me what they think I'm doing wrong," Kane told the chief. Cavanaugh was a fair and reasonable man. There had to be a way to get the chief to agree to let him go solo.

"Agreed," Brian replied genially. Then amusement curved the corners of his mouth. "Which is exactly why I'm not assigning you to partner with one of the department's German shepherds."

Brian leaned back in his chair and gestured first toward Kane, then toward his grandniece whose performance was at times a little bit unorthodox. But by all counts she was both professional and tenacious— and she got results, which was what he was ultimately shooting for.

He smiled at her now, just before saying, "Detective Kane Durant, meet your new partner, Detective Kelly Cavanaugh."

Durant's expression never changed, Kelly observed, but she thought she saw a flicker—just for a moment—in the other man's eyes that told her the thirty-two-year-old detective was far from happy about this newest coupling that was taking place.

"I'm not an unreasonable man," Brian went on to say. "If this partnership isn't working for either one of you after, say, a couple of months, you can request a reassignment and I'll consider the matter. Nothing is written in stone," the chief went on to assure the duo.

"But before either one of you decides to make that request, I want you to give this partnership a decent try." He emphasized the words *decent try*. "Remember, nothing worth keeping comes easy. The rewards that are the sweetest are those that are hard-won." Deep green eyes swept over both detectives, one at a time. "Do I make myself clear?" he asked.

"Perfectly," Kelly replied with all but unbridled enthusiasm.

"Yes, sir," Kane said. His low-key voice was all but flat.

Satisfied, Brian nodded. "Good. Now good luck— and goodbye," he added. Just like that the meeting was over.

Kane lost no time leaving the chief's office. Walking briskly through the outer office, he headed straight for the elevators.

Kelly found she had to lengthen her stride to keep up with her new partner. The latter gave absolutely no indication he *wanted* her to catch up.

He certainly wasn't willing to slow down long enough for her to accomplish that small thing.

Too bad, she thought, lengthening her stride with determination.

Kelly arrived at the elevators just after her new partner did.

The man was going to take some getting used to. Right now, he seemed to be all blustery, like a bull confined in the proverbial china shop. He couldn't seem to turn around without knocking something down and breaking it.

The worst part, she thought, was that he was aware of what he was doing—and not even the most subtle display of remorse was forthcoming from the man. There was obviously a good reason for that—he was feeling no remorse. Or, if by some chance he actually was, he was exceedingly careful not to show it.

He wasn't like the other detectives. Something had made him different. It was up to her to make different synonymous with extra capable. Her grand-uncle saw qualities in this man, she could tell. She'd heard that Brian Cavanaugh had never been wrong when it came to doing what was best for his police force.

Although she was somewhat skeptical about this particular arrangement working out, Kelly decided she was just going to have to proceed on faith.

"How do you want to do this?" she asked her new partner brightly, breaking what was beginning to feel like an ironclad silence. Kane had given absolutely no indication he would say *anything* if she didn't prod him into it.

"'This'?" Kane echoed. The elevator arrived and he stepped inside. He noted how she seemed almost to hop in, claiming the space directly next to him.

Terrific, the chief had assigned him to partner up with a rabbit, Kane thought darkly. A chipper, bright-eyed and bushy-tailed rabbit.

The idea did not inspire him.

"Yes," she confirmed. After almost a minute went by, she realized that her new partner didn't have a clue what she was referring to. So she elaborated. "You have your desk and I have mine," she pointed out.

"So? Is this where you tell me something informative about desks?" he asked with more than a touch of impatience in his voice.

"So one of us has to make a move. Amos cleared his desk out before he left," she told him, hoping that Muhammad would opt to come to the mountain rather than deal with the mountain coming to him. "Your partner did the same when he transferred out of Robbery and into Vice," she concluded.

Kane looked at her sharply. Just how closely had this eager little beaver been paying attention? His most recent partner, Woodward, had abruptly just picked up and left. Since the chief of ds had known all about it, Kane assumed Woodward had left with the man's blessings—his didn't count, even though he'd made no secret that he was glad to be rid of the man. Until just now, he'd had no idea where the detective had gone, nor had he cared, as long as it was away from him.

He just assumed it would be the same deal when it came to his current partner. A few weeks would go by—maybe even the two months to which the chief had referred—and then his newest so-called partner would bolt, and he would be more than glad to be rid of her.

But for now, he had a question he wanted answered. "How do you know which division Woodward transferred to?"

"I pay attention," she answered simply. She waited for Kane to answer her question about which of them would be transferring desks, but that didn't look as if it was about to happen. She began to doubt he was even listening to her.

In that case, the man had a serious attention deficit disorder. She tried again, since it was obvious that what she considered to be a possible dilemma didn't seem to have occurred to her new partner at all.

"Okay," she began again. "Now, do you want to switch desks or should—"

A curt "No" cut her down midsentence. Trying hard not to look annoyed, Kelly tried another approach to pin the man down.

Was he saying no to everything or just to the first part of her sentence? Kelly dug deep for her patience.

"Do you mean no, you don't want to switch desks? Or no, you don't—"

Kane cut in as if she wasn't saying anything—at least nothing worthwhile. "You want me to hire a skywriter? Would that help you understand?" he asked impatiently.

Words rose to her lips that would only fan the flames and turn this into a full-fledged raging forest fire. She practiced restraint—although it was far from easy. She settled for sarcasm.

"No need to go to that expense. Just use your words, Durant. Do you want to move?"

"No," he bit off. "I don't want to move."

There was nothing to be gained by echoing his sentiment and saying she didn't want to move, either. One of them had to and, apparently, at least for now, she had been awarded the role of the flexible one.

"Okay," she agreed gamely. "Then I'll be the one to move."

Kane wanted to say no to that as well, but he knew he couldn't, not without consequences. When the chief of ds said he wanted him to give the partnership two months, the man *meant* two months. So, for now, he was forced to go along with this most unlikely, not to mention unsuitable, coupling.

"See, that wasn't so hard now, was it?" she asked, employing a cheerfulness she definitely wasn't feeling. Just for good measure she decided to add, "Wait and see, we'll have you talking in full sentences in no time."

Kane's eyes narrowed as he momentarily glared at her just as the elevator doors opened again, this time on their floor. Kane got out. She was quick to follow him.

"Although," she continued as if they were actually carrying on a conversation instead of what was mostly a monologue on her part, "there is something to be said for silence, too," she admitted, carefully avoiding getting on the wrong side of Kane's dark expression.

She was bending over backward. This was *not* going to be easy. But then, her late mother had told her more than once that she had the ability to get along with the devil.

The devil, Kelly silently contemplated, turning the thought over in her mind. That definitely would go a very long way toward describing her new partner's disposition.

Who would have ever thought that the devil was this handsome?

A small smile played along her lips. Who'd known her mother had had the ability to look into the future?

Now all she had to do was prove the rest of her mother's statement right.

Chapter 2

"Good, you're back."

The abrupt greeting came from Captain Lawrence Collins, a ruddy-faced man of medium height who was currently in charge of the robbery division. He'd come out of his office the instant that Kane and Kelly had walked into the squad room.

Kane glanced at the stocky man with his fading red hair, but said nothing in response to his greeting. Clearly, he was waiting for the man to continue.

However, it wasn't in Kelly's nature to just sit back and wait when she could just as easily jump into the middle of whatever was going on.

So she did.

"Did you want to speak to us, Captain?" she

asked, more than eager to sink her teeth into a case. Her last case had been closed right after Amos's retirement party and she was itching to get involved in something that could, just possibly, bring her and the sphinx she was assigned to a little closer together.

Probably not, but a girl could dream, Kelly thought whimsically.

"Want to? No," Collins retorted. The bags under his eyes, Kelly noticed, seemed extra deep today. "What I want is to find some way to retire and enjoy myself the way I'm sure Barkley's doing right now." The captain sighed, acting more put-upon than weary. "But that's not going to happen for another ten years, so in the meantime I get to hand out assignments to hotshots and hope for the best."

Collins hesitated for a moment. He looked tempted to hand the piece of paper he was holding to her, but after several seconds of what appeared to be deliberation, he turned over the paper where he had jotted down all the pertinent information that had come in and handed it to her new partner.

Just as well, Kelly thought. Durant most definitely had a chip on those big broad shoulders of his, and if the captain had singled her out to take lead on this new case, Durant probably would have felt slighted. He had, after all, been with the department longer than she had. And if it appeared that Collins favored her over Mr. Congeniality, she had a feeling the end result would be less than pleasant.

This way was better for both of them.

"Looks like you two just caught your first case together," Collins told the pair. "Make me proud," he added as he nodded at the paper he'd just given Kane. He began to walk away, then stopped in his tracks for a few seconds. "Oh, and, Durant?"

After reading the address written on the white notepaper, Kane looked up and waited for the captain to continue.

"See if you can hold on to this partner for longer than a month, okay? The paperwork that's generated every time you break up with your partner is hell," Collins complained as he made his way back to his office.

This time Kane's eyes slid over the woman who had hurried to catch up to him and was currently standing less than an inch away.

"I'll do my best," Kane murmured more or less to himself.

"Do better than that." Collins apparently had heard Kane's comment despite the growing distance between them as he walked back to his glass-enclosed office.

To Kelly's momentary surprise, Kane turned around and walked out of the office again. She found herself hurrying again just not to lose sight of him.

The sooner they got to the location the captain had handed over to Kane, the sooner they could start working on the case.

"Is that your personal best?" Kelly asked him as they went out again.

"Is *what* my personal best?" Kane asked brusquely. What the hell was she talking about? The woman apparently could jump from topic to topic faster than a frog touching down on a pond filled with burning lily pads.

"A month. With a partner," Kelly added as clarification since Durant wasn't answering her and gave no indication he planned to. Not if that disinterested look he'd just sent her way was any indication. "Is that the life expectancy of a partnership with you?" she asked.

Kane shrugged, apparently totally uninterested in her choice of topics or her edification as to his professional habits.

"Give or take," he finally replied vaguely, aware of the way she was watching him, waiting for an answer. "I don't keep track," he added with an air of finality that was meant to close the subject once and for all.

Or so he had naively thought.

Kelly nodded. "Fair enough," she told him. Then she explained, "I just wanted to know what I was up against, that's all."

His eyebrows drew together in an outward sign of confusion. "What's *that* supposed to mean?" Kane asked.

She gave him a roundabout explanation. "I'm

planning to look at this partnership as a challenge. If I can hang on beyond a certain point, say longer than your longest-lasting partner, then it's okay. I made it. You know, kind of like staying on a bucking bronco for eight seconds."

If the woman wanted a challenge, he had one for her. He'd challenge her to make sense out of the gibberish she had just spouted. Instead, though, he settled for a throwaway line that he assumed would tell her just how disinterested he was in anything she had to say beyond whatever pertained to the case they were about to investigate.

"Whatever floats your boat," Kane muttered dismissively.

"Where are we going?" she asked as they got back on the elevator.

"To the scene of the robbery," he told her matter-of-factly.

If he was trying to rankle her or get her to lose her temper, Kelly thought, it was going to take more than that. Having grown up with four brothers, not to mention two sisters, she had learned how to survive under adverse conditions.

"Which is…?" she asked him patiently.

He seemed deliberately to wait several minutes before saying, "Quail Hill."

Kelly whistled, impressed. For the most part, the citizens of Aurora were middle-class and upper middle-class. But Quail Hill was where the beautiful people with deep pockets lived.

After reaching the first floor, the elevator came to a stop and opened its doors. The moment they stepped out, Kane resumed his quickened pace, letting her know in no uncertain terms that he didn't like the idea of being coupled with her. He was putting distance between them as quickly as he possibly could. She was welcome to keep up—if she could.

Too bad, Durant, but I don't like this any better than you do, she thought, once again lengthening her stride.

"Well, if I was a thief, that's where I'd go to pull off a heist," she said, addressing Kane's back. "The really filthy rich part of town."

Kane merely grunted in response as he came to a stop before a dark sedan. He hit the release button on his key, opening all four doors simultaneously.

Kelly looked at his vehicle in surprise. He seemed to take it for granted that she was just going to let him take over every little aspect of their partnership.

"That's it?" she questioned. "No discussion about which car we're using and who's driving?"

Rather than answer her, Kane opened the driver's side door and got in behind the steering wheel.

"I guess not," Kelly concluded, answering her own question.

Opening the passenger side, she slid in. The moment she inserted the metal tongue into the slot of her seat belt, Kane took off. Kelly felt the jolt. The sedan was instantly hugging the road, doing the speed limit—and just beyond.

Kelly gave it to the count of ten in her head, allowing her new partner to gather his thoughts together before he said something.

Anything.

When there was only silence riding along in the car with them, Kelly decided that the man she'd been assigned to was comfortable with this level of silence.

She, however, was not.

"You know, you're going to have to talk to me sometime," Kelly pointed out patiently. There was no point in raising her voice or losing her temper. That wasn't the way to go with this man.

Kane continued looking straight ahead as he drove onto one of the city's main thoroughfares.

"Why?" His voice was steely, his interest in the conversation barely engaged.

Exasperation hovered around the edges of her voice, but Kelly managed to keep it in check.

"Because that's what partners do. They talk. They share and somewhere in between the small talk and the theory spinning, they solve crimes."

"If you say so," Kane responded in quite possibly the most disinterested, distant voice she had ever heard. "But it's cliché."

She wasn't trying to be original, just to make a

point. There was nothing wrong with using a cliché if it applied to the situation—and this, in her opinion, did.

"I've got another one for you," she told Kane, her stubborn streak rearing its head. "Ever hear the old saying, 'Two heads are better than one'?"

"You planning on growing another head, Cavanaugh?" he asked.

If he meant to get her annoyed with that, he was going to be disappointed, she thought.

"Was that a joke, Durant? Could it be that you actually have a sense of humor buried beneath that muscle-bound, hulking exterior?" she asked, feigning shock as she splayed her hand across her chest.

He merely slanted a dismissive look her way before returning his gaze to the road.

Taking a deep breath, Kelly decided she had nothing to lose by taking this new partner of hers to task about his attitude when it came to her. "Look, Durant, I don't know what your problem is—"

He pointed up to the rearview mirror. "Mirror's right there," he said, his meaning clear.

Kelly dug in. "Subtle. Wrong, but subtle. I'm not your problem, Durant," she told him. "I'm not the one who's had six partners bail on her since joining the force."

"Five," he corrected, looking, in her estimation, completely unfazed.

"I'm not convinced that it was getting shot that

made that partner of yours to decide to take a different career path, but if it makes you happy to believe that, fine," she said. "The count is back down to five."

It was obvious that she was deliberately humoring him, the way an indulgent parent humored a child. He didn't like it.

"What would make me happy," he told her, feeling his jaw clench as he spoke, "is if you said goodbye."

Okay, maybe it was time to take this head-on, Kelly thought. Sidestepping and humoring this man weren't getting her anywhere.

"What is it that you think you've got against me?" she asked. "You hardly know me."

"And I'd like to keep it that way," Kane told her in no uncertain terms. "Having a partner—*any* partner—just gets in my way," Kane said in a no-nonsense voice. "I don't have time to watch your back."

Rather than get angry—or throw her hands up and just give up—Kelly tried another approach. It was obvious the man was keeping something buried. Something that had caused him to become soured on life as well as the world.

She aimed to find out what that was.

"And you don't have time to have your own back watched?" Kelly asked.

He laughed shortly. There was absolutely no humor in the sound. "No offense, but if I were in trouble, knowing you were out there with a gun wouldn't exactly reinforce my feeling of well-being," he told her.

Kelly stared at his rigid profile. It looked as if his whole body was clenched, not just his jaw. Did the man even *know* how to relax? Or was he just perpetually angry at the world?

Why?

She had nothing to lose by asking. Heaven knew she wasn't sacrificing any rapport she might have built up with Durant. There certainly wasn't any to be had.

"Were you *always* like this?" she asked. "Or did something happen to turn you into this distrusting outsider?"

That was the deal breaker. If she didn't put in for a transfer, then he would—the moment they got back to the precinct, Kane promised himself. "And just about the very last thing I need or want is a partner who fancies herself a shrink."

"Not a shrink," Kelly contradicted. "An observer. Someone to talk to when things get to be too difficult for you."

It seemed as if he was missing every single light, Kane thought, gripping the steering wheel harder. Missing the intersection lights just made his disposition that much more surly.

"What if *you're* what's too difficult for me?" he asked.

She smiled, the expression filtering into her eyes, making them all but shine with warmth.

Now why the hell had *that* thought even crossed his mind, Kane upbraided himself.

"We can talk about that, too," Kelly told him.

The look he shot her was not the sort that cemented partnerships. "Got an answer for everything, is that it?" he asked sarcastically.

"Pretty much," she said, giving no indication that his attitude was getting to her.

Something—or someone, she decided—had done a number on this new partner of hers, very effectively destroying his ability to relate to anyone. To *risk* relating to anyone, she amended.

Either that or he was just an ornery SOB and there really was no reaching him.

The moment she started to consider the second possibility, Kelly quickly dismissed it. Nobody on earth would want to be the way Durant was on any kind of a regular basis, Kelly thought. Something *had* to have happened to him to make him like this.

But what?

And how did she find out? Heaven knew she couldn't approach him outright about that. At least, not without proper prep work first.

She made up her mind to do some digging into her new partner's past and see if she could answer any of the questions that were popping up rather insistently in her brain.

Kelly began planning her strategy and who she would talk to first about Durant. A number of possibilities occurred to her, along with another thought. She was going to make Kane Durant her private rehabilitation project.

Lost in thought and making extensive plans, she didn't immediately become aware that Durant had stopped driving.

After parking his sedan at the curb, he got out and then spared her a glance. Against his better nature, he prodded her.

"Coming?" he asked her. "Or are you waiting for a private, hand-carved invitation?"

Kelly didn't lie as a rule. But she saw no shame in shading the truth sometimes, especially when she was dealing with someone such as Kane Durant, a man who probably had last smiled on the day he'd been brought home from the hospital.

Possibly not even then.

"Just gathering my thoughts together," she told Kane cheerfully. She did, however, avoid his eyes when she said it. That, and she devoted an extra drop of care to getting out of his sedan on the passenger side.

"Well, that certainly doesn't require a long time," Kane commented under his breath.

She ignored the obvious meaning behind his comment—that her thoughts were woefully few. "No, not at this time," she easily agreed.

She could see that her noncombative answer surprised him.

Brace yourself, Durant. There's more where that came from, she promised silently. *I intend to kill you with kindness. It's probably the only way to win you over.*

Or so she hoped.

A patrol car was parked at the end of the long, winding driveway. The vehicle looked sadly out of place beside the two other cars that were there. One was a late-model Mercedes and the other was a Lexus that was so new it didn't have plates on yet.

Both cars had been vandalized. Their windows were smashed and huge red letters scarred the body of each vehicle.

"Looks like someone was taking out some really dark personal issues on the cars," she commented. "Maybe they were using the cars as proxies for the people the perp or perps *really* wanted to harm."

Very quietly, Kane slowly circled the two cars, taking in every inch of the destruction that had occurred here, so close to home. At first glance, it seemed like a case of determined vandalism. But there might be something that they were missing, he thought.

That was why the department had such a highly developed crime scene investigation unit. "Ask CSI to pass on their findings to me—to us," he corrected himself, although not overly cheerfully, "once they're finished examining the cars," he instructed.

Kelly nodded her head. "Consider it done," she replied.

Kane glanced at her and appeared on the verge of responding. Then he obviously thought better of it and merely shrugged his shoulders.

Taking in everything about his surroundings, Kane continued walking to the building's ornate, massive front door.

The door was wide-open. A patrolman could be seen just inside the foyer. He seemed to be on guard. Against what was still unclear.

The foyer, a veritable shrine to all things marble, contained uncommonly high vaulted ceilings. It clearly gave the impression of wealth as well as wide-open spaces.

"God, I'd hate to have to pay the heating bill on this place," she murmured as they walked in.

Kelly hardly knew where to look first. She was accustomed to nice houses, but this was a whole new frontier. She was impressed but determined not to sound like some highly impressionable schoolgirl.

"What do you think it runs them?" she asked in idle curiosity. "The heating bill," she repeated so Durant knew what she was talking about.

For a moment, she'd forgotten who she was paired up with. The question was something she would have asked Amos. The latter would have speculated about the price and offered a decent guess. That was what she had loved about Amos. She could engage him in any sort of topic and he would always try to keep the conversation going.

This new partner didn't even indicate that he had heard her question.

She glanced around and took in the security system keypad that was mounted right inside the door. "Looks sophisticated," she commented.

"Also useless if it didn't alert the home owners that an intruder or intruders were coming in," Kane pronounced rather dismissively.

She was about to say something along the lines of "He speaks" but immediately dismissed the urge. She wanted to encourage Durant to share his thoughts with her. If she said anything remotely mocking or derogatory, she knew it would only make matters that much worse.

And completely blow any chance of a decent partnership right out of the water.

She also had a feeling that at this stage of their nonrelationship, kidding him was not the way to go. Instead, she played her role as the faithful sidekick and asked innocently, "Think it might be an inside job? You know, maybe someone who had a hand in installing the security system?"

"Too soon to think anything," he told her as he continued moving around the foyer, taking in as many details as he could before going to speak to the home owners. Both were badly shaken, according to the initial report that had come in from the patrolman who had been the first on the scene.

The home owners were not difficult to locate. Kane followed the sound of raised voices and crying into the next room.

...the...

Chapter 3

The woman's back was to the doorway, so she didn't seem to be aware that anyone else had entered her home—and her living room—until she heard an unfamiliar, deep male voice say, "Excuse me."

No doubt surprised and frightened, Judith Osborn jumped and stifled a scream as she swung around toward the sound of the voice she heard, apparently much to her husband's disgust, if the expression on his face was any indication.

"Damn it, Judith, get hold of yourself. They're obviously with the police." Randolph Osborn's small, deep-set brown eyes shifted back and forth between the two strangers who had entered his home, as if he was assessing them. "You *are* with the police, right?"

Kane took out his wallet and badge at the same time that she did. Kelly let him do the introductions as she continued to study the pair. The wife's nerves seemed to be very close to the surface, while her husband just looked angry. Very angry.

"Detectives Durant and Cavanaugh," Kane told the robbery victims. Closing his wallet, he returned it to his jacket pocket. "Are either of you hurt?" he asked even as he did a quick visual check.

Neither seemed to be bleeding, which was a positive sign.

Osborn fisted his hands and then relaxed them again. His frown—as well as his annoyance—appeared to be deepening. "I think I lost all feeling in my hands and my back's killing me."

"We can call the paramedics if you like," Kelly offered sympathetically. Her focus was more on Mrs. Osborn than on the woman's husband. The latter had an irritating manner about him, which might or might not have been due to finding himself the victim of a robbery. Kelly had a feeling it went far deeper than that. "They can take you to the hospital to be checked out."

Osborn looked at her as if he thought she'd lost her mind to make such a plebeian suggestion.

"What? Checked out by butchers? No, thanks. I have my own top-rated specialist on retainer." Wearing a robe over his pajamas, Osborn began to head for the nearest extension. "I'd like to call him now if you're finished here."

He was summarily dismissing them.

Kelly could see that Kane didn't like the man's superior attitude any more than she did.

"As a matter of fact," Kane told the home invasion victim, "we're not finished." He put his hand down on the landline Osborn was about to dial. "We have a few questions we'd like you to answer."

"What more do you want from us?" Mrs. Osborn asked, an edge of hysteria rising in her voice. "We've already told that…that beat cop standing outside what happened. What else is there?" she demanded again, her voice breaking.

Judith Osborn ran her hand along her throat, as if she was protecting herself from some sort of invisible noose hanging around her neck. That was when Kane noticed the ligature marks around Judith's wrist. Picking up the hand closest to him, he examined it more closely.

It didn't take much to guess what had happened. "You were restrained," he concluded.

Judith timidly pulled her hand away as she whispered hoarsely, "Yes."

At the same time her husband spat out, "Damn right we were. That little vermin had us tied up like turkeys waiting to be slaughtered," he proclaimed indignantly. "I want that bastard's head on a platter and I want it *now*!" It was clear he intended to get exactly what he demanded—or he was going to make someone else suffer for what he had gone through.

"I can understand you feeling that way, Mr. Osborn," Kane told the man, sounding *almost* compassionate. "But that's not quite the way we do things on the police force these days."

The expression on Osborn's face all but shouted that he didn't give a damn how the detectives did things. *He* wanted revenge for being humiliated and held prisoner in his own home. "Then after you bring him in, just let me have ten minutes with him—"

Kane saw the same set of ligature marks on Osborn's wrists. "Looks to me as if you've already had more than ten minutes with him."

Accustomed to always getting his way, Randolph was obviously fuming at Kane's comment. He made a show of pulling the cuffs of his pajamas down over the marks on his wrists.

To Kelly it was a little like the clichéd remark about closing the barn door after the horses had been stolen.

"He came into our bedroom while we were asleep. Our *bedroom*!" Osborn all but shouted to get his point across. "And he had the *gall* to hit me to wake me up!" His wife whimpered pitifully as Osborn recreated the scene they had just gone through. "Then he had my wife tie me up. My *wife*," he emphasized. Osborn glared now at the woman who, it was quite evident by his manner, he felt had betrayed him.

"I *had* to, Randolph," Judith cried, distraught. "He was holding a gun on me. What did you expect me to do?" she asked. The almost painfully thin woman began to shake again.

"I expect you to *think* for a change," Osborn retorted. "If you had given him *any* sort of resistance, I could have used that to get him off guard and taken his gun away from that pathetic sack of—"

"What you would have more likely taken," Kane said, interrupting the abrasive man he was taking a real disliking to, "is a bullet, most likely to the stomach. And you would have bled out before we got here. Heroics don't usually pay off," he told the man matter-of-factly.

Osborn ran his hand through his graying hair. "I don't need to stand here and be lectured to by a two-bit detective," he bit off angrily.

"Well, it's obvious that you certainly do need something," Kelly said, cutting in. Her eyes met Osborn's. Kelly didn't look away. "A course in manners comes to mind."

"You can't talk to me like that," Osborn shouted at her.

"It seems that I apparently just did," Kelly replied with a wide, genial smile that was anything but.

Osborn began to breathe hard as he clenched his impotent fists next to his sides. "Do you have *any* idea who I am?" he demanded.

"Yes," Kane replied in an even, controlled voice.

"You're a citizen of Aurora who has been robbed and as such you and your wife will get our full attention. There's nothing to be gained by throwing your weight around. That doesn't impress us. As a matter of fact, that really doesn't work in your favor."

"Did either one of you get a look at this guy—there was only one, right?" Kelly wanted to ascertain. She was doing her level best to get the couple's attention back on the robbery and not on some high-spirited exchange between Kane and the male victim.

Judith bobbed her head up and down, a wreath of carefully salon-dyed brown hair floating about her face. "Yes. One. One *horrible* man." She shuddered, running her hands up and down along her arms.

"Can you remember any physical features?" Kane pressed.

Judith shrugged. One of her nightgown straps slid down. She nervously tugged it up into place again, glancing in her husband's direction as she did so.

Osborn was the one who ran the show, Kelly concluded. Mrs. Osborn gave them a description. "Average build, average height. Around Randolph's age—"

"Which is the same as yours," her husband bit off, taking offense that she had made it sound as if he was older than she was.

In response, Judith looked down at the rug, avoiding his eyes.

"Was there anything familiar about this man?"

Kane asked. "Anything at all? The way he spoke or held his head? The way he moved around, perhaps?"

"Familiar?" The haughty inquiry came from Osborn. "We're not in the habit of fraternizing with common burglars and thieves. Besides, the bastard wore a mask."

"What kind of a mask?" Kane asked, hoping to gain some insight into the burglar's mind-set.

"It was a clown mask." Kane noted that the man was most obviously holding himself in check to keep from allowing a shiver to snake down his spine. "I've always hated clowns. They're grotesque."

"Can't argue with you there," Kane replied almost under his breath as he made a further notation in his notepad. "Have you had a chance to assess what the robber made off with?"

"Two very rare paintings and an antique revolver I kept on display there." Randolph pointed to the credenza in the dining room. The stand on top of it was glaringly empty.

"Were the paintings down here, too?" Kelly asked.

Judith bobbed her head up and down in response to the question.

"They were the first thing anyone saw when they came into the house," Osborn answered bitterly, gesturing to the vacant spaces on the wall. The only things that testified to the paintings' existence were two nails in the wall.

"Did he take anything else?" Kelly asked the angry home owner.

"No." He shook his head. "Just the paintings and the revolver."

She realized the man hadn't been outside to see his vandalized automobiles. Just as well right now, she told herself.

Despite Osborn's answer, Kelly went down a list of popular items to steal—and fence. "No jewelry or expensive bottles of wine or—"

She didn't get to finish her list. Osborn was glaring at her as he rudely interrupted. "What part of 'no' don't you understand, Detective?"

She was tempted to say something cutting that would put the man in his place, but considering the trauma he and his wife had just gone through, Kelly decided to cut him a little slack.

She turned toward her partner and bounced a theory off him. "Wouldn't it have been easier just to take the paintings and the antique gun and disappear without bothering to wake up Mr. and Mrs. Osborn?" It seemed to her a far easier way to proceed as well as to avoid possibly getting overpowered and caught.

"Yes," Kane agreed thoughtfully. After a beat, he added, "Unless—"

"Unless he *wanted* them to be alerted to what he was doing. He wanted to rub their noses in it," she concluded, excited about this possible twist and its implications. Turning back to the home invasion victims, she asked Osborn, "Is there someone who would want to watch your reaction to the robbery? Maybe even take some pleasure in it?"

"The people at the club are all a bunch of jealous bastards," Randolph spat out. "Any one of them could have done this."

"No." The nervous denial came from his wife. "They're our friends."

Osborn shot his wife a furious, disgusted look. "If you believe that, you stupid cow, you're even more pathetic than I thought."

"There's no need to get abusive, Mr. Osborn," Kane coldly informed the man, stepping between Osborn and his wife.

"I can get whatever the hell I want with my wife. I've just been robbed, and I sure as hell am not going to be lectured to by one of the Keystone Cops."

It was Kelly's turn to step in. She was beginning to realize it was going to be hard narrowing down the list of people who hated Osborn's guts and wanted to see him humiliated. Undoubtedly, it was a non-exclusive, fast-growing club.

"I'd be very careful if I were you, Mr. Osborn," Kelly warned the man in what sounded like a very deceptively mild voice. "Or you just might wind up reaping exactly what you sow."

"What's *that* supposed to mean?" Osborn angrily demanded.

Kelly didn't bother explaining. "You're a very

smart man, Mr. Osborn. I'm sure you'll figure it out on your own eventually. Now then, we'll need a list of all these 'unfriendly' friends you think might be capable of breaking into your home for the opportunity to torture you by robbing you. Also an exact accounting of everything that was stolen."

It was clear that Osborn was about to say something less than cooperative, but Kane cut him off before he could speak.

"When you finish with the list, you can give it to Officer Riley," Kane told the man, pointing out the officer to him. He was fairly certain that although the officer had undoubtedly introduced himself to Osborn when he'd arrived on the scene, the latter had taken no note of his name, or even thought the man *had* a name.

The officer was now standing guard just inside the foyer.

"And where are *you* going to be?" Osborn demanded in less than genial tones. He sounded like an employer wanting an accounting from a lowly lackey.

"We'll be off working your case," Kane replied, the picture of restraint.

The only telltale sign of inner fury was that Kane's breathing pattern had grown just a little bit shorter.

Kelly held her tongue until after they'd taken their leave. The minute they were outside the front door, Kelly's words came rushing out.

"Wow. For a minute there I thought you were going to strangle him," Kelly told him. "Not that anyone in the immediate world would have blamed you. That man was some piece of work."

"If I strangled him, I might have done the world a favor," Kane speculated. In his opinion, Randolph Osborn was a colossal waste of flesh.

"No argument," Kelly agreed. "It's just that you might have had to fight me for the honor of bringing about the man's demise." She shook her head as she looked over her shoulder at the twenty-room house. "Makes me think that this so-called robbery was definitely *not* just a random act of chance."

Kane sounded her out. "You think someone targeted him?"

She couldn't tell by Kane's tone if he agreed with her or not. All she could do was tell him how she felt about the crime.

"With every fiber of my being," she said with enthusiasm. "It only makes sense." Her voice picked up speed. "Whoever did it wanted to see Osborn agonize over losing his precious treasures. There's no other reason why he would have deliberately woken Osborn and his wife up, tied them up and then dragged them downstairs to bear witness to the robbery. It was most likely someone Osborn belittled or stiffed in some deal—or both. I'd bet my pension on it," she concluded.

"Which probably amounts to fifty dollars a month

at this point in your career," Kane said dismissively. "As to it being someone Osborn had wronged somehow, it looks like that club includes everyone over the age of three. That's a hell of a lot of people to question," Kane concluded.

"There has to be a way to narrow down the list," she told him.

Kane frowned as he reached his vehicle. Offhand he couldn't think of a way to accomplish that. He glanced in her direction as he sat behind the steering wheel. "I'm open to suggestions if you have them."

Getting into the passenger side, Kelly shook her head. "Right now all I can think of is that I'd like to strangle the condescending, smug, giant creep myself."

For a second, Kane allowed himself to be amused. She was almost cute when she got angry. Now there was a word that shouldn't ever be paired with the word *partner*. He knew without being told that if he said as much to her—that she was cute when she got angry—there would be hell to pay. Something to think about, he mused, "Tell me, does that go above or below the part that says protect and serve?" he asked.

She took no offense at his so-called question.

"I'll let you know when I figure it out." She turned her attention to another detail in the investigation. "Those marks on Mrs. Osborn's wrists looked pretty deep," she commented. "You think that whoever is responsible for this has a grudge against her, too?"

He shrugged. "It's possible," Kane allowed. "Or maybe, for our suspect, it's a matter of guilt by association. She's married to the miserable reptile, so in the burglar's mind she's every bit as bad as her husband is."

She nodded. "Could be that, too," she agreed.

"Let's see what their so-called friends at the club have to say about the Osborns," he suggested, then Kane looked at her. They were currently missing one little detail. "Did Osborn happen to mention what club he belongs to?"

She shook her head. "There are four clubs in Aurora that a man like Osborn might want to belong to. My vote is with the one that's the most exclusive—and the most snobbish."

Kane knew the exact place. "Valhalla," he said. "That's the one that checks into your lineage before allowing you to join. Members had to have relatives that go all the way back to the Mayflower." He saw the frown on Kelly's face. Out of left field, the thought came that even when she was frowning, this pain in his posterior was damn attractive. He promptly buried it, forcing himself to focus on the case. He caught himself wondering if she knew something he didn't.

"What?"

She waved a hand at his question. Her reaction

had nothing directly to do with the case. "I just hate snobs."

"If your hunch is right, then apparently the snobs have the same kind of feelings about Randolph Osborn and his wife."

Satisfied that they might be onto something, Kane put the key into the ignition. The engine had trouble catching the first two times. The third try was the charm. The sedan dutifully purred into service.

Kelly nodded toward the front of the car. "You should have that looked at," she suggested.

Kane shrugged dismissively. "It's just being temperamental."

That he was assigning feelings to the vehicle took her completely by surprise. "It's a car," Kelly pointed out. "It doesn't have any emotions to govern its actions."

"My car might disagree," he told her, completely tongue in cheek.

Kelly found herself laughing. "If you had a car that was actually *capable* of disagreeing, you'd be at least ten times more wealthy right now—if not more—and definitely living the life of ease."

Money, and its lack or presence, didn't play a role here. Not for him.

"If I were wealthy," he told her, "I'd still be doing exactly what I'm doing right now. Protecting and serving. And chasing bad guys."

The admission caught her completely off guard.

She hadn't pictured him as being *that* dedicated. "You're kidding."

"I don't kid," Kane deadpanned.

The way he said it, Kelly caught herself thinking that she could really believe it. But it was what he said next that really threw her for a loop.

"Cavanaugh."

She turned her head to look at him, waiting for what she assumed was most likely going to be a put-down.

"Nice work back there."

Stunned, for a moment she had absolutely no comeback for that.

Chapter 4

Was that a compliment?

Seriously?

Kelly looked at her solemn partner in barely contained astonishment.

"Excuse me?"

"You heard me the first time," he told her flatly.

"Actually, I did," Kelly admitted, then smiled broadly at him when his glance toward her turned accusatory. "But it has such a nice ring to it. Humor me and say what you said again."

Kane blew out a breath as he shook his head. Served him right for going soft for a second. So far, none of what transpired was convincing him that partnering was a good way to go for a man such as him. He returned to his original belief: There was no upside to having a partner. Definitely no upside to having a crazy partner.

"You're a real pain in the butt, Cavanaugh. You know that?" Kane accused her.

Kelly pretended to seriously mull over his words. "No, I don't think that's what you said. It was something about my having done good work."

Scowling at her, Kane continued to face forward, his eyes on the road. "Keep this up and you'll negate any good effects you managed to accomplish."

Kelly merely laughed as she shook her head. "You are a very tough crowd to please, Durant."

He was beginning to think this woman he'd been stuck with would drive him crazy inside of a week. He didn't do his best work agitated. One way or another, there would be a breakup in their future—and very soon.

"I don't know what the hell that means," he growled. "But I'm not going to ask."

"It means—"

Still driving, Kane took his right hand off the steering wheel and held it up much the way an old-fashioned traffic cop directing the flow of vehicles would have.

"I said I'm not going to ask. That implies that I don't want to hear you dissecting your own words. In case you're unclear on the concept, that means—"

"Okay, moving right along," she quipped, interrupting his explanation and calling a halt to that line of conversation. With a sigh, Kelly looked out the window at the road before them. For the first time she took note of the route he was taking. It was a different one than they had taken to the high-end residential community. "Are we going directly to the club?"

This time Kane didn't even bother glancing in her direction. "What does it look like?"

She had a great deal of patience, but it was in finite supply. This man had to be put on some kind of notice, she thought. Otherwise, this testy behavior was liable to continue for days.

"It looks like one of us should seriously think about stopping by the hospital to have a boulder-sized chip removed from their shoulder," she told him in a sweet, matter-of-fact manner that not even the most critical of people could find fault with.

"Then, once that chip is removed, maybe we'll have a shot at working together a bit more smoothly." Or at least she could hope that would be the outcome of the proposed venture, Kelly silently added.

The look he gave her was far from happy or even mildly approving. "This is as smooth as it is going to get."

"You underestimate yourself," she told him. Adding, "As well as me."

He'd tried, he'd really tried, Kane thought. But there was a time when you just had to recognize that the deck was stacked against you. It was time for him to cut his losses and just withdraw.

"I have no estimation where you're concerned," he told her in a distant, removed voice. "As for me— no offense—but I just don't like having a partner."

"None taken," she responded cavalierly. "And I kind of picked up on the fact that you are less than thrilled about this arrangement. But you know what, Durant? There's a reason the department sends their detectives out in pairs, so you might as well get used to it."

She didn't think he would come up with an answer so fast, but he did. "It cuts down on the number of cars they have to provide."

She stared at his profile, rather amazed at the way Kane's mind worked. "Wow, you really *are* cynical, aren't you?"

He continued watching the road as he went. "Never claimed to have a sunny disposition."

And this woman was nothing if not a Pollyanna, Kane thought. Pollyannas required a happy, hopeful atmosphere around them. That just wasn't him and it never would be.

"If you want to ask for another partner, I won't contest it," he said.

"Contest it?" she echoed. Just how dense did the man think she was? "You'd probably break into a happy dance." The momentary mental image of the solemn, handsome detective suddenly swaying to some melody only he heard had Kelly grinning. "And that is something that I would actually pay to see," she admitted. "But not enough to break up this beautiful friendship we've got going here between us."

"What beautiful friendship?" he all but growled.

"The one I'm laying the groundwork for," she replied cheerfully. "Pay attention, Durant. And FYI, I'm not a quitter. That means that I don't take off at the first sign of a problem—or the promise of a difficult partner," she deliberately added. "You're just going to have to get used to that.

"So, if you were hoping to get rid of me by giving me a sample of your sunny disposition, sorry, it's not going to happen. By the way, the answer to the question that I asked you earlier about why the department pairs up detectives, it's so that they can have each other's backs. I figure you're too good a cop not to have mine, and I sure as hell am going to have yours," she told him in no uncertain terms.

"As for the rest of it, you want to sulk and behave like some dark and brooding character out of one of Byron's poems, go right ahead. Be my guest. But you'll be missing out on some pretty terrific conversations," she predicted.

The look he spared her was nothing if not skeptical. "Meaning with you?"

If he was trying to get her to back down or to intimidate her, he was going to have to work at it a lot harder than that, she thought. "I don't see anyone else in the car. So, yes, meaning me."

Kane laughed shortly. "Think a lot of yourself, don't you?"

She raised her chin ever so slightly, which was the only indication that she might have found the question combative.

"What I just said has nothing to do with whether or not I think a lot of myself. I just happen to know my strengths *and* my limits. That's all.

"And if you're wondering," she continued, "I have inside knowledge—no pun intended—on the way the male mind works. I grew up with four brothers who were anything but docile. They supplied me with my education, and I diligently took notes," she told him completely straight-faced.

Without her realizing it, they had arrived at Valhalla.

After Kane showed his badge, the man at the club's entrance reluctantly opened the gates to allow them to drive on to the grounds.

"Let's see if you can put those so-called notes you took to good use," Kane challenged her as he headed to the clubhouse.

The route to the impressive structure was marked with a great many expensive, well-cared-for vehicles. The most conservatively priced of the lot turned out to be a silver Mercedes.

"Never understood it," she murmured, taking in the sea of pricey automobiles. The comment was more to herself than her partner since she just assumed Durant wasn't paying attention to a word she said, anyway.

Kane surprised her by asking, "Never understood what?"

She managed to recover without missing a beat. "Pouring so much money into something that could so easily be totaled in the blink of an eye. Whether a car's a Ford or a Ferrari, they're both just a heartbeat away from becoming a mangled heap."

Kane shrugged. Expensive cars meant nothing to him. They'd never moved him, not even as a young boy. Life had been far too serious for him to be infatuated with an automobile.

"They're status symbols, I suppose," he said.

She took in the groups of golfers on the course just before they reached the clubhouse. "I know that, but this crowd doesn't strike me as the type to be impressed by someone dropping a quarter of a million on a Lamborghini."

Thoughts of his father suddenly popped up in his brain. On those rare occasions when his father hadn't been taking out his frustrations on him or his mother, his father had told him that if he ever won the lottery—the one that he was always faithfully buying tickets for—the first thing he'd intended to do was buy a fancy car. The kind that would make everyone sit up and take notice.

"I'd get my due respect then," he'd said. "Not like now."

Usually right after that, the scenario would disintegrate into his father blaming everyone else for his misfortunes. And shortly after that, Kane would be on the receiving end of a particularly vicious beating. That had seemed to be the only way his father could cope with the events in his life, by taking out all his frustration on either his wife or his son. Or both.

Thinking of that now, Kane regarded the pricey vehicles. "You'd be surprised at what does the trick for some people. To some people, it's all about the kind of vehicle they drive. The flashier, the better."

Not him, Kelly thought. Durant wasn't the type to go for flashy status symbols. She would bet on it.

But someone in his life, past or present, had valued flashy status symbols, she decided. She could tell by the way his tone had changed when he'd mentioned it.

Kelly waited half a beat before falling in step directly behind Kane. She meant for him to go first. To her surprise, he deliberately slowed his pace just enough to allow her to catch up.

She was about to thank him, then decided that Kane probably didn't want her thanks. The less said on the subject, the better was probably the way he liked it. He was going to cause her to reevaluate her whole approach to partnerships, Kelly mused.

"Is there something I can do for you?" a very tanned, very polished looking man in his midforties asked politely as he walked up to them. His clean cut looks and the touch of silver at his temples, in addition to his manner of carrying himself, all pointed to him as being someone in charge.

And he was.

"Detectives Durant and Cavanaugh," Kane said, taking out his wallet and holding it steady to allow the man to have a closer look at his identification. Kelly did the same. "We were wondering if you could tell us if one of your members—a Randolph Osborn—was friendlier with any one of your members than he might have been with some of the others."

"Leon Edwards," the man introduced himself. "I'm the director here." He got back to the question that had been put to him. "Friendlier?" Edwards questioned, clearly amused. "You *are* asking me about Randolph Osborn, correct?"

"We are," Kane confirmed, clearly waiting for a more precise answer.

The director seemed to gauge his words carefully. Memberships and high revenues in the form of donations were at stake here.

"Mr. Osborn, I'm afraid, wasn't what you would call *friendly* with any of the members," Edwards said stiffly. "He did associate with a few of our members, if that's what you mean."

Kelly stepped in, knowing her partner would take that as an affront. Kane, she was beginning to see, didn't exactly have the gift of diplomacy. He favored the direct approach rather than attempting to sugar-

coat his words. The man obviously never had sub-
scribed to the old philosophy of catching more flies
with honey than with vinegar.

"Could you give us a list of the members' names?"
Kelly requested.

Edwards looked at her and it was obvious to Kelly
that he liked what he saw here better than he did
when he was interacting with Kane. But there were
still rules he obviously was obligated to follow.

Edwards's gray eyes shifted from one detective
to the other. "Just what's this all about, detectives?"

"Mr. and Mrs. Osborn were the victims of a home
invasion last night," Kane informed the director
matter-of-factly.

The man's eyes widened from their customary
slits. Edwards appeared genuinely surprised. "Was
anyone hurt?" he asked.

Kelly could tell that her partner was going to give
the director a flat "no" in response. It hurt nothing to
give Edwards a crumb, feeding his obvious need to
get something exclusive on the man, however minute.

"Only Mr. Osborn's pride," Kelly confided, low-
ering her voice as if she was sharing something that
deserved to be labeled a secret.

"Well, I can understand that," the man replied,
bobbing his head up and down. And then, as if
his brain was on some sort of ten-second delay, he
looked up at the two detectives before him, clearly

stunned. "And you two think that someone *here* is responsible for that home invasion?"

That was stating it too blatantly. Kelly decided to reframe her answer so that it sounded more as if they were working with a turn-of-the-last-century mystery. "We think someone here can possibly give us a clue or some sort of a lead as to who might have wanted to do this to the Osborns."

"You mean break into their house and steal something from them?" Edwards asked. "I assure you that—"

"No, we mean someone who might have wanted to humiliate Mr. Osborn," Kelly was quick to correct the director's misimpression.

She glanced at Kane, then made up her mind that allowing Edwards to learn a little bit of the truth would help them close this case sooner rather than later.

"We believe that whoever did it could have easily gotten in and out with the Osborns sleeping right through the entire ordeal, none the wiser," Kane said. "The objects of the theft were on the first floor and the Osborns' bedroom is on the second.

"But they were roused, tied up and made to sit through the robbery. The thief obviously wanted to observe their humiliation firsthand. Would you know of anyone here that Mr. Osborn might have had words with? Or maybe there was someone harboring ill will against him for some reason?" Kane supposed.

"Some*one*?" Edwards echoed with a smirk he

didn't bother hiding. "Would you like those names alphabetically, chronologically or listed by the size of the offense?" the director asked them.

"That many?" Kane marveled. Even he hadn't expected this to be turned into a crowd scene, which was the way it was clearly heading.

The director looked to either side of him as if to see if there was anyone within earshot.

Apparently satisfied that he wasn't going to be overheard, Edwards confided to the pair, "You didn't get this from me, but that man never met an argument he didn't like. It is getting to the point that the board is seriously considering asking Mr. Osborn to relinquish his membership if he can't learn how to get along with the other members.

"It would definitely be a shame to revoke their membership since everyone likes his poor, long-suffering wife." And then Edwards's face sobered as he focused on the subject. "But Mr. Osborn is making it very difficult for us to turn a blind eye to his irritating manner. We *do* have to think of the other members…"

Kane glanced at her and Kelly could see by the look in her partner's eyes that Kane felt the director had given them way more information than they wanted regarding the man in question.

More is better than less, Kelly had decided a long time ago.

"Absolutely," Kelly heartily agreed. "Mr. Edwards,

we don't want to make your job any more difficult or challenging than it already must be, but we could really use that list of people that Mr. Osborn has had differences with." When the director continued to look reluctant to comply, Kelly added, "We *could* get a warrant making you give us that list, but that would call a great deal of unwanted attention to your club. You don't need that sort of publicity now, do you?"

"No, of course not," Edwards answered, his tan growing a few shades lighter right before her eyes. "All right. If you have something to write with, I can give you that list right now."

"You don't have to check your records or surveillance tapes?" Kane questioned suspiciously.

In response, the director tapped his temple. "All the records are right here, and I can access them whenever I want. That way there's no fear of someone hacking into our database and making off with some—shall I say?—less than favorable information."

"Understood," Kelly said, humoring the man. Then, just for good measure, she added another layer of sweetener. "This club is certainly lucky to have someone like you running the place."

The director beamed and wrote faster—just as Kelly suspected he would.

Chapter 5

"You thinking of applying here?" Kane asked her once she had the club director's list in her hands and they had walked out of the clubhouse.

Surrendering the list to her partner, Kelly looked at him, her expression clearly indicating that he *had* to be kidding. She wouldn't have been caught dead associating with people who acted superior to anyone who didn't bring in a seven-figure salary. Being around a group such as that was her idea of hell.

"What makes you ask something like that?"

"The way you were playing up to the guy, I figured you were trying to create a favorable impression so you could ask to fill out one of their applications."

Kane's disapproving expression made it crystal clear what he thought of belonging to a club such as that.

After reaching the sedan, Kelly got in. "I was playing up to him, as you so eloquently put it, to get that list without having to go plead our case in front of some ADA who then would have to get a judge to sign off on the warrant. Making nice with the director was the faster route to take," she pointed out.

Kane put on his seat belt and put the key in the ignition, but he left it there for a minute. He wasn't finished just yet.

"What's the problem with getting an ADA and a judge to back us up? Correct me if I'm wrong, but don't you people have both in your extended stable of family members? You could have a warrant sent to your email faster than it takes to talk about it."

Kelly frowned as she raised her eyes to his. She was trying to control the sudden surge of temper she was experiencing. Generally easygoing to a fault, she found that this new partner could get to her faster than even her brothers could, doing their worst—and that was saying quite a lot.

"Just because they're in the family doesn't automatically mean that we can use family to bend the rules," she informed him.

"Right," he answered loftily. Kane didn't believe that any more than he believed the Golden Gate Bridge was for sale. About to start the car, he spared her another glance. She didn't belong here. She was too pretty, too distracting. He wasn't some rutting pig, but he was human after all.

Right now, Cavanaugh looked as if she could shoot darts from her eyes—with him as the target. "Wait, you're serious?"

"Damn straight I am. Just because the power is there doesn't mean it's there to abuse."

Looking more amused than convinced, Kane said, "I guess I stand corrected."

Her easygoing disposition didn't mean she had been born yesterday. Kelly read between her partner's lines. "But not convinced."

Kane shrugged. The old adage about Rome not being built in a day crossed his mind. "I'll get there," he told her cavalierly.

Kelly took what she could get. "Fair enough, I guess. Let's find out just how many of these people coveted Osborn's paintings."

"'Coveted'?" he echoed. Shaking his head, Kane started the vehicle. "You're invoking biblical terms now?"

She took no offense at his tone. "Think of it as broadening your educational base."

"My base is just fine, thanks," Kane informed her. Kelly noticed that for once he didn't sound curt. Was she making progress? Or was it just an oversight on his part?

"There's always room for improvement," she

maintained. Then, just in case he took that as a personal criticism, she added quickly, "For everyone."

He awarded her a long, scrutinizing look before looking back at the road.

"Some more than others," he agreed, and she knew he was referring to her.

A freshly minted, snappy comeback hovered on her lips, straining to be released. But they weren't going to get anywhere if this exchange degenerated into one-upmanship. One of them *had* to be the bigger person and just back off.

Kelly blew out a breath.

In this case, she supposed that for the sake of progress and future harmony, it was going to have to be her.

The list of Osborn's so-called friends included ten names. Three of the people were currently on the premises.

"They actually track their members when they're on the club grounds," Kelly had marveled in mild disbelief.

One of the members could be found in the dining area—specifically at the bar, while the other two were on the immaculately kept golf course, apparently trying to lower their handicaps.

"Since we're here, might as well talk to them first," Kane decided.

* * *

An hour later they were back in Kane's sedan, none the wiser or further along in their investigation than when they had first arrived at the club.

"Seven more to go," Kelly said with a sigh, dropping into the passenger seat and closing her door. "Who knows? We might get lucky. Seven's a lucky number, right?"

"So now you're superstitious?" Kane asked as he started his car again.

"What I am is trying to stay positive. Approaching this with a negative attitude isn't going to get us anywhere. Although I have to say that talking to those people makes me feel as if I need to take a shower."

She looked at her partner's almost rigid profile, wondering if the man ever relaxed. He had exceptional bone structure, but right now she was looking at a museum statue, not a flesh-and-blood man.

"I never knew that men were capable of being as catty and vindictive as women," she confided, trying to get some sort of a response from Kane. Getting him to act human required far more work than she'd anticipated.

"It all depends on their maturity level," he commented, guiding the vehicle through the grounds and heading for the exit. "The men we talked to had a combined emotional age of about sixteen. Possibly less."

"I guess having a lot of money doesn't always buy you peace of mind. Sometimes all it buys you is acrimony," she theorized.

Kane looked at her sharply. "Back up. What did you just say?"

"What? You weren't listening?" Kelly cried, pretending to be both surprised and offended. "And here I thought you hung on my every word."

Kane snorted. "More like I could hang you for uttering too many words," he replied before repeating his question. "Now what did you just say?"

To be honest, she wasn't really sure what she had said exactly. Certainly not something that should have had him reacting this way. She tried to think and came up with something. "That I didn't know men could be as vindictive as women."

He waved away the words as if they were solid entities. "No, after that."

Her thoughts seemed to run together. "That these men were full of acrimony. I'm paraphrasing it, but—"

But Kane shook his head impatiently. "Before that," he instructed.

She wondered if he was coming unglued or if he was just trying to make her crazy. After again reviewing her earlier words, she came up empty. With a shrug, she told him, "I really don't know what you're referring to."

He tried to catch the sentence himself, but failed. "Something about money—"

It almost came back to her. "That it was supposed to buy peace of mind?" It was more of a question to check if that was the phrase he was trying to recover.

For a split second, Kane lit up like a veritable Christmas tree. By the time he said, "Right!" his face had returned to its regular, somber expression.

"O-kay," she drew out, having no idea what her partner was driving at. "And this particular little set of words is important to you because…?" She waited for Kane to fill in the blank space.

"Because it made me realize that we need to look at Osborn's financials," Kane told her.

She nodded, game. "Anything in particular that we're looking for?"

"We're going to see if Osborn is as financially secure as he'd like the world to believe he is." Enthusiasm surging through him, Kane took the turn a little too sharply. Kelly braced her hand against the glove compartment to keep from sliding on to the car's floor.

She stared at Kane for a minute, and then it was as if she could suddenly tap into his train of thought. *Now* it made sense. "You're thinking Osborn orchestrated his own home invasion because he needed the insurance money he'd get for the paintings if he claimed they were stolen."

The moment she said the words out loud, she was convinced this actually could be a viable possibility.

"It's true what they say," Kelly said. "Desperate men do desperate things. The thief gets to fence the paintings and the antique pistol, while Osborn gets to collect on the insurance money. As far as he can see, Osborn probably views this as a win-win situation."

Even though it was his theory, Kane wasn't entirely sold on it. There was a sticking point that bothered him.

"Osborn did look genuinely angry about being robbed and tied up." He reviewed another point from a different angle. "I supposed that for a large lump sum of money a lot of people would be more than willing to put on a believable act."

Her partner sounded as if he was arguing with himself. She was tempted to ask if he was engaged in a private fight, or if it was it open to everyone, but at the last minute, she thought it might be useful to get the plan of action straightened out.

"So we don't talk to the rest of his so-called country-club buddies?"

Kane glared at her as if he couldn't figure out where she had gotten that idea. "We'll still talk to them, but the more options we consider, the better our odds of solving this thing."

Kelly nodded, doing her best to remain positive. "That sounds good to me."

"Oh, good, now that I have your blessing we can proceed."

She allowed annoyance to slip over her features. There was no point in trying to keep it all in. She'd probably wind up getting an ulcer if she kept going this route. So she gave Kane a piece of her mind, something she wouldn't have considered doing before.

"You know, up until just now, I was beginning to really admire you," she told Kane.

Getting her to keep talking, Kane felt he might get some further insight into the way her mind worked. It was never too late to try something new—and giving her a partial kid-glove treatment was definitely something new for him.

"And now?" he challenged.

He could be really arrogant if he wanted to be, Kelly thought. And he obviously wanted to be this time around. "And now all I can say is you're lucky we're not standing by the edge of a pool because you'd find yourself suddenly needing a change of clothes."

He inclined his head as if he was taking all of this in, unfazed. "And you'd find yourself on the wrong end of a murder charge."

"What are you talking about?"

"If you pushed me into a pool, you'd be guilty of homicide."

She stared at him. How did he figure that? "I don't follow your—"

"I can't swim," he told her in a flat voice.

"You're a Californian," she reminded him. "Of course you can swim."

Damn but she could be obtusely stubborn if she wanted to be, he thought. "Contrary to what you seem to believe, Californians are not born with gills and water wings attached to their bodies. Nor are they born with the ability to immediately tread water."

"You really can't swim," she marveled in compete disbelief.

Since she had been the one he'd used as an unwitting sounding board, he felt he had to cut her just a tiny bit of slack. So he repeated it one more time. "I really can't swim."

"Why didn't you ever learn?" she asked, still having trouble processing the idea that someone who lived in an area where he could go swimming year-round hadn't learned how to swim. Her father had been adamant that she and all her siblings learn by the time they went to kindergarten.

"Can we just drop this?" he said. It was not a request.

"Okay," she allowed. "But if you ever decide you want to learn how to do a few simple things that'll keep you afloat, I'd be more than happy to teach you. It could save your life someday," she added on.

The look he shot her as he took a right turn told her that the man obviously thought he'd be a fool to put his life in her hands by taking her up on her offer.

Out loud he said, "I'll get back to you on that." His tone indicated it would be slightly ahead of when hell was scheduled to freeze over and become a skating pond.

Three hours later, back in the squad room and slowly going cross-eyed, she heard Kane bite off a few choice words. Looking up from the computer search she was conducting, Kelly took a semiwild guess as to the source of his less than jovial mutterings.

"I take it that the financial angle didn't pay off the way you thought it might?" she asked.

"Not really," he admitted. "Osborn made a few bad investments and his accounts have gone down some in the last year, but nothing major. Certainly nothing that would compel the man to suddenly mastermind stealing his own paintings."

She could see that Kane appeared somewhat disappointed about this last turn of events. "Well, it was a good idea," she told him, then added, "Too bad it didn't pan out."

The sentiment she expressed had Kane laughing rather drily. There was no humor in his voice or in his eyes.

"The road to hell is paved with good intentions," he said in disgust.

Now he was just throwing phrases around for the sake of throwing them, she thought. "And there's a connection there how?"

"None," he admitted after a beat. "I'm beginning to babble like you." He seemed rather appalled at the mere suggestion he was behaving in a similar manner.

She smiled brightly at him. So he *was* reachable.

"Knew there was hope for you," she told Kane. "Feel like taking a break from all this—" she gestured at the laptops on their desks "—and talk to some snobbish rich people?" Although, she added silently, she'd welcome another kind of break with this strong, silent type. A break that had nothing to do with law enforcement and everything to do with getting to know her partner better. *Intimately* better.

Knock it off, Kelly, she ordered herself. They had a case to solve, not an itch to scratch.

He sighed and got to his feet. Her invitation sounded anything but promising, much less interesting. But right now no other options were on the table.

"Might as well. This isn't getting us anywhere," he grumbled, nodding at the computer screen and the records he'd managed to access.

Kelly never lost a step as she hustled to keep up with him.

Questioning the rest of the people on the list they

had obtained from the country-club director proved to be just as frustrating and fruitless as the rest of their day had been.

"Did the CSI people come up with anything yet?" Kane asked her after the seventh interview had gone the way of the other six they had conducted, marathon-style.

She tried to find a comfortable spot in the passenger seat. "Not that I know of," she said, feeling very tread worn. It took her a second to realize what was bothering her about his question—she really was pretty tired. "And wouldn't they call you about that and not me? After all, you're the primary on this case," she pointed out.

"And you're the relative," he countered. "And that usually trumps anything else."

She knew he was referring to the fact that the head of the day crime scene investigation unit was Sean Cavanaugh, another one of her newly discovered granduncles as well as the chief of detectives' older brother. At times, that might seem a little daunting if not downright overwhelming, but all it took was dealing with these people to realize that they weren't part of some secret club, they were all just people on the same team: law enforcement.

"Again, that would be going against protocol, otherwise known as *the rules*. If anything, I might get a heads-up at the same time as you do—although that's highly unlikely," she emphasized. "But they wouldn't get in contact with me and not you. It doesn't work that way," she insisted. "The only advantage I have as a Cavanaugh is if I ever get shot, or need a kidney, odds are there's a relative who could step up and donate their blood or their kidney or whatever."

She took a breath and then said in an even voice, "I'm only going to say this once, Durant, so listen up. Same name or not, none of us will ever capitalize on the fact that we're related. Having the same last name doesn't open up doors for us so much as it opens us up to be the target of a great deal of criticism and misconceived ideas." She gave him a very pointed look as she said this.

And then she brightened.

"Okay, the subject is now closed." Kelly glanced at her watch. "It's past our shift." Way past, she thought. "What do you say that we get some dinner? And since it's my suggestion, I'll spring for it. Sky's the limit—up to ten bucks," she deadpanned.

He wasn't thinking about food right now. Unwinding was what was currently on his mind.

"Thanks for the offer, Cavanaugh, but I'm going to drink my dinner."

"Smoothies?" she asked, summoning her best innocent look. She knew damn well he wasn't thinking about combining a handful of healthy ingredients in a blender.

Kane laughed shortly. "What do you think?"

She gave it to him straight. "I think that you need

a designated driver coming with you. Wouldn't do to get a DUI, considering your career choice."

He took chances when he was out in the field, but only in the line of duty. No way he intended to drink and drive. "I was planning on picking up a bottle and taking it home with me."

The thought of him sitting alone in his apartment, helping alcohol evaporate out of a bottle filled her with a strange sort of sadness. "You can always do that some other time."

"Is this what it's going to be like?" he asked. "If we, through some perverse trick of nature, actually remain partners, are you going to argue with everything I say?"

She wasn't aware of being argumentative right now, just helpful. "Not argue," she corrected, "I'm tactfully suggesting alternatives."

He frowned. "You're not exactly making the best argument for my staying your partner."

"On the contrary, I'm making a great argument for remaining your partner."

He looked at her for a long time. "I've died and gone to hell, haven't I?"

"Nope. If anything, it's the other place."

He sighed, giving up. He drove into the police parking lot and stopped by her car. She was coming with him tonight, he knew that without being told. Just as he knew that wherever he went, she was going to follow, like a shadow he had no control over.

Chapter 6

Located not far from the precinct and inherently inviting, Malone's was thought of as more of a tavern than a bar. The difference boiled down to the crowd that tended to congregate within the family-owned establishment.

All manner of law enforcement agents—although the balance tended to lean toward officers and detectives—came to Malone's seeking a little respite from the burden of keeping the city and its residents safe. The tavern was a place to go when someone needed to blow off a little steam, or seek the company of like-minded people, or just remain silent while listening to brethren in blue talk and attempt to make some sense of the madness around them.

In addition, at any given time of the day—but especially in the evening—a good dart game could always be found.

Kane had been to Malone's a handful of times, but for the most part, if he sought relief, he did it in the confines of his own living quarters rather than in the middle of a crowd of people who shared his calling.

His idea of blowing off steam did not involve talking or competitive dart throwing.

The upshot of that was Kane had no overwhelming desire to go to Malone's.

However, he was beginning to realize that if he didn't make at least a minor show of going along with his new, hopefully soon-to-be-ex partner, he would get absolutely no peace until he finally *did* go along with her—at least for a small amount of time.

Which was why he wound up going to Malone's with her at the end of his day.

The moment Kane walked through the front door, the heat generated by having so many bodies milling around in what was actually a relatively small space hit him with a jolt.

Malone's appeared to be filled to maximum capacity—and it wasn't even a Friday or Saturday night.

"Looks like there're a lot of partners here," he commented.

Kelly hadn't thought the tavern was going to be *this* crowded, but she was quick to adjust. It was a trait she had acquired in her formative years. If nothing else, life with six siblings demanded constant adjustment and she had gotten good at that.

"Partners?" she questioned. That was rather an odd way to put it. At times Kane could be very difficult to follow. He probably did that on purpose, to keep her off balance.

Which meant that she had to rise to the challenge.

"People partnered with a Cavanaugh," Kane elaborated for her benefit. "I figure that'll drive anyone to drink every time."

Ah, sarcasm. How could she have missed that, Kelly wondered. "Very funny."

"I wasn't trying to be funny," Kane told her. "Just factual."

There wasn't a hint of a smile evident on his face or in his voice. Still, she preferred to think that Kane was joking. That way she wouldn't take offense at his words—the way she secretly suspected that he might want her to.

I'm not rising to the bait, Durant. Sorry.

"Well, then, I'd say you had a lot in common with these people," she concluded cheerfully. "Why don't you go and mingle a little? I'll be here when you're ready to go home."

"I'm ready now," Kane informed her flatly.

"You left off two very crucial steps before the final one," Kelly pointed out. "You forgot all about the drinking and the mingling parts."

"You might not have picked up on this," Kane told her testily. "But while I do drink, what I don't do is mingle."

"Neither did the Unabomber," she reminded him. "And we all know how that turned out. It's a fact of life, Durant. People need people," she insisted

That sounded suspiciously like a lyric to an old song his uncle's lady friend used to sing. Kane was instantly on guard. "I swear, Cavanaugh, you break into song and I'll strangle you right here, witnesses or no witnesses."

"Then it's lucky for you I forgot my sheet music," she told him sweetly. She caught hold of Kane's arm and began to pull him to the counter.

Caught off guard, Kane allowed himself to be pulled rather than to cause a scene. Since the place was this crowded, he had no doubt the Cavanaughs were well represented. He also had no doubt they'd be quick to defend one of their own and he had no desire to get into the middle of anything like *that*.

"What's your pleasure?" Kelly asked him as she reached the bar and raised her hand to attract the exceedingly busy bartender's attention.

"Home," he answered.

Kelly decided to ignore her partner's response.

The bartender had managed to cross over to her at that moment and she gave the retired officer the name of a beer she happened to know he carried on tap. "Two," she told the man.

Kane looked at her in mild surprise. "I thought you said you weren't drinking."

"Just the one," she told him. "It just doesn't seem right, taking up space and not buying something from Devin."

The name meant nothing to him. "Devin?"

She nodded, saying, "The man who just took our order. It's his bar. Well, his family's bar," she amended. "They're all former cops."

He thought that was rather fitting under the circumstances. "The job'll drive you to drink, all right," Kane agreed. He looked pointedly at her as he said it.

Kelly returned his look and smiled at him. She was determined not to allow the man to get to her.

"You'll get no argument from me," she told Kane, her eyes on his.

Just then someone bumped into Kane, throwing him off balance. Before he could do anything to stop himself, Kane bumped up against his partner.

The tavern was unusually warm and the space exceedingly tight. Kelly had her back against the bar, so she had nowhere to move when Kane bumped up against her.

For a split second it felt as though their two halves had sealed and formed a whole. The kind that created electricity and caused lightning bolts to shoot into space.

The kind that made Kane acutely aware of the contours of his partner's body, as well as of his own.

Slightly shaken, Kane blamed his reaction on his surroundings, on the stressful day he had just put in and just possibly on the fact he felt trapped in more ways than one. Those were all the components he felt justified in blaming for the very intense way his body had reacted to hers.

It wasn't Cavanaugh he was reacting to, Kane silently and fiercely insisted. It was the circumstances, nothing more. In the absolute sense, she *was* an attractive woman.

And he wasn't made out of wood.

Kane wound up polishing off the glass of beer she had ordered without even realizing that he had raised it to his lips.

Watching him, trying to distract herself from the very intense way her body had reacted to his, Kelly asked, "Another?"

Kane was on his guard immediately. "Another what?" he asked.

Kelly indicated the empty glass on the counter in front of him with her eyes. "Are you up for another glass of beer?"

"I haven't even finished the one I have," Kane protested.

"Yes, you have," Kelly contradicted.

About to argue the point—what was her game, anyway?—Kane looked down at the counter and saw that his glass had been drained.

"Oh."

It was official, he thought. The woman was making him so crazy, he was oblivious not just to his surroundings, but to everything he was doing, as well.

Pushing his glass closer to the bartender, he said, "Okay, why not? One more." After that, he silently promised himself, he would go home—even if he had to take a cab.

The second the words were out of his mouth, Kelly raised her hand, waiting for the bartender to look her way again.

But when the man came over to where they were standing at the bar, it was Kane who put down a ten-dollar bill on the counter.

"Another round," he told the man his partner had called Devin.

"None for me, Dev," Kelly demurred, putting her hand over the mouth of her glass. "I'm driving."

"Understood," Devin told her, then he glanced at her partner.

But Kane was looking back at her. "One more won't hurt," he told her, adding, "Worse comes to worst, we share a cab."

"Tempting," Kelly allowed, even though, if she were being honest, it really wasn't tempting to her in the slightest.

She drank beer to be social, not because she actually cared for its taste. When it came down to drinking because she liked the taste, she preferred the kind of drinks her brothers made fun of. The fruity tasting

drinks that came with tiny umbrellas and a smatter-
ing of fruit floating on the surface.

"But I'll have to pass," she told her partner. "I
don't like leaving my car unattended in a parking
lot overnight."

After a moment, Kane nodded. "Yeah, I see your
point." Although crime was down considerably, it
was far from wiped out. A car left unattended all
night in a parking lot represented a great deal of
temptation. "You'd think that the city's finest could
find a way to keep their own vehicles safe."

His eyes were still holding hers.

Kelly was aware of what he was trying to do.
Kane was trying to get her to back down—or maybe
back off. She was not about to do either.

"I'm sure they're working on it," she said, standing her ground. "Get me a ginger ale, Dev," she requested. "So I have something to hold in my hand."

Ginger ale, she reasoned, was the same color as
some of the beer that was flowing tonight. Given
the dim lighting, she figured that would be a good
substitute.

No doubt aware of what she was trying to do,
Devin winked at her. "You got it, pretty lady."

She grinned, then said good-naturedly, "You're
already getting a tip, Dev. Go chat up someone else."

The bartender laughed. Dispensing the ginger ale
into a mug, he placed it on the counter in front of her.
"On the house," he said, then turned toward Kane.

"Be good to her," Devin told him before he moved on to answer the call of another customer.

"What was that supposed to mean?" Kane asked her. Did the bartender think something was going on between him and Cavanaugh? Where the hell had he gotten that impression?

"Maybe Devin's telling you not to strangle me," she quipped just before taking a long sip from the mug the bartender had served to her.

"He didn't seem that intuitive," Kane responded. "Unless, of course, he's spent time with you."

Kelly looked at him over the rim of her ginger ale. "You are a regular laugh riot," she told Kane. "If you ever decide to leave the force, you might consider a job as a stand-up comedian."

"I don't like crowds," he reminded her.

"Don't worry," she told him cheerfully. "There won't be any when you perform."

He was about to retort, then decided to dial back his response. Instead, he inclined his head and said, "Touché."

The next moment, a tall, dark-haired man with a genial smile made his way over to them and began to talk as if he had been standing at the bar with them from the beginning.

"This your new partner?" Brennan Cavanaugh asked his younger sister.

If she was surprised to see him, Kelly gave no indication. She nodded in response to his question.

"Durant, this is one of my brothers, Brennan," she said, introducing her partner to her brother, and then reversing the order. "Brennan, Kane Durant."

Before Kane could say a word in response, Cavanaugh's brother had taken hold of his hand and was pumping it heartily.

The moment the wide smile appeared, Kane saw the family resemblance.

"My sister driving you to drink already?" Brennan asked with a laugh.

"After the day we just put in, I thought he deserved to spend a little quality time at Malone's," Kelly informed her brother. "I'm only here because I'm his designated driver."

There. That should take care of any speculation on Brennan's part that this might be some sort of a date or something.

Her brothers were always trying to pair her off with someone, especially since Valri, their baby sister, was now officially engaged and off the market.

She wondered if they were doing the same thing to Moira, her other sister.

Brennan turned and eyed Kane in astonishment. "And you agreed to this arrangement? Having her drive you home?"

"She more or less agreed for me," Kane replied. The only say he'd had in the matter had been uttering the word "Yes."

"No" had not been an acceptable word to use at

the time and clearly wouldn't have computed even if he had said it. "Why?" Kane asked.

Brennan answered his question indirectly by turning to Kelly and asking her a question. "Has he seen you drive?"

"Not exactly," she hedged. Only one block separated Malone's from the police precinct. Brennan laughed as he clapped his hand on her new partner's back, finally getting back to the man's question.

"I'd say you were in for a treat, Durant, but I'd be lying. If you have a rosary, I'd suggest clutching it. It might afford you some measure of comfort." Before turning to leave, he had one final suggestion. "Also, closing your eyes would probably help."

"Brennan," Kelly began, a warning note in her voice.

Obviously wanting to distract his sister from reading him the riot act, Brennan looked down at his watch. "It's getting late. Gotta run. I promised someone dinner," he told Kelly with a wink. Turning toward his sister's partner, he told Kane, "Nice meeting you. Hope this isn't the last time."

With that, Brennan headed toward the front door and quickly disappeared into the crowd.

"He didn't mean that," Kelly was quick to tell her partner.

He wasn't all that sure he knew what she was referring to. "What, that it was nice meeting me?" Kane asked.

"No, that he hoped this wasn't the last time he'd see you. And for the record," she added, "I don't drive nearly as badly as Brennan was trying to imply. He never got over being my big brother, which made him utterly overprotective."

But Kane wasn't about to be distracted from the topic he had honed in on. "Just how badly do you drive?"

"I don't." Realizing that he might misunderstand what she was telling him, Kelly tried to clarify her statement. "What I mean is that I don't drive badly." Then, for the sake of honesty, she felt obligated to admit, "But I do drive a little fast at times."

Kane nodded. He had nothing against that. A little speed was a good thing.

"A *little* fast?" Kane questioned approximately forty-five minutes and three more beers later. They had finally left the tavern and Kelly was taking him home.

She had just narrowly squeaked through two yellow lights that both had been in the process of turning red. In addition, she had taken a right turn a tad too quickly, all but completing the hairpin turn on the passenger side's two wheels.

Kane had been entertaining a slight buzz as they'd walked out of Malone's. That buzz was now completely gone, evaporated in the heat of what he felt was very justifiable fear.

"If you ask me," he said to her, his hands braced against the dashboard, his body rigid to keep from falling to the side. "Your brother didn't begin to scratch the surface with his warning. You drive like a crazy woman," he told her.

"That's just the beer you're feeling," Kelly told him.

"No, that's just reality I'm feeling," Kane contradicted. "Pull over," he instructed, intending to take the wheel. "Thanks to your driving, I am fully sober now and more than able to drive myself the rest of the way home."

She spared him a quick look, then focused back on the road ahead. If she recalled correctly, there was a tricky maneuver just up ahead.

"Too bad," she told him. "This is my car, so I get to drive. Just take a deep breath and you'll be home in no time."

Her words gave him no comfort. "Home as in my apartment, or as in the afterlife that priests and ministers all talk about and on occasion refer to as 'home'?"

Kelly laughed as she shook her head. "As in your apartment," she answered, refusing to be baited. "Did my brother really manage to get to you?" she asked, surprised. Kane didn't seem like the type to be spooked easily.

"No, but your driving is," he told her.

Again he braced his hands against the dashboard

in an effort to try to steady himself as she took another corner quickly.

"For your information," she informed him. "I haven't had an accident yet."

That was one statistic he intended to follow up on. "I guess that's enough to get me to start believing in miracles," he replied.

"And here's another one," she concluded with a grand gesture of her hand as she indicated the area outside his side of the vehicle. "You're home."

Surprised, Kane looked out the windshield. She was right.

Chapter 7

To his surprise, Kelly got out of her vehicle at the same time he stepped out on the passenger side.

"What are you doing?" he asked. He saw no reason for her not to drive off.

"I'm surveying the property," she cracked. "What does it look like I'm doing?"

"You're walking me to the door?" he asked incredulously. There was so much wrong with this picture he wasn't sure where to start.

She snapped her fingers. "You figured out my secret. I'm walking you to your apartment," she confirmed. When he gave her a very skeptical look, she added, "I don't mean to imply that I think you can't hold your liquor. Let's just say I'm satisfying my curiosity as to where you live." She smiled up at him brightly as she fell into step beside him.

"It's not some dark cave, if that's what you're thinking," he told her.

With that he pointed toward the garden apartment located just beyond a central planter. The flowers in the planter seemed to be fighting a losing battle, she noted as they passed.

She laughed at his description. "Never even crossed my mind. No stairs?" she asked as he stopped before the door of a ground-floor apartment. She'd pictured him as someone who preferred being closer to the sky than to have someone living over him.

"I like being close to the ground," Kane told her as he fished out his keys.

"Fear of heights?" she guessed.

When he answered her, she noticed that Kane neither denied nor confirmed her guess. Instead, he said, "It's easier to hit the ground running this way."

What he meant by that escaped her for the moment. She noticed that Kane tended to wax a little philosophical now that he had more than three beers in him. There were worse things, she decided.

Holding the key in his hand, Kane refrained from putting it into the lock. He supposed that a few parting words were in order.

"I'd invite you in—"

The next word he was about to say was *but*, however he didn't get a chance to utter it because that was when Kelly said, "Okay," and moved a bit closer to him, as if she was waiting for the door to be opened.

"But," Kane continued with determination. "I'm not set up for company."

He was the *last* person she would have thought felt uncomfortable about the appearance of his living quarters. "I'm not company," she told him. "I'm your partner, remember?"

"I'm trying very hard not to," he told her with a degree of honesty.

Kelly continued talking as if he hadn't interjected anything. "That makes me like family," she concluded, making her point.

His eyes were flat as Kane countered, "Not *my* family."

Something in his voice caught her attention. But she couldn't quite put her finger on what about it bothered her.

She watched his face as she asked, "Why? No girls in your family?" It was a guess at best.

Kane didn't answer her.

He hadn't been all that open with her tonight, but now it seemed as if a barrier had come down between them.

Hard.

"I'll see you in the squad room tomorrow," he said, turning away from her.

"Oh, you'll see me before then," Kelly informed her partner.

He'd just inserted the key into the lock and glanced at her over his shoulder. He kept his hand protectively over the doorknob.

"Why?" Kane challenged. If she was planning on meeting him for breakfast somewhere before their shift began, she was out of luck. This was as much fraternizing as he intended on doing for the rest of the year. Perhaps longer.

"Because I'll be driving you in," she said, trying to rouse his short-term memory. Kane had executed a perfect three-point turn to successfully parallel park, taking full advantage of the space closest to the six story precinct building. Right now, however, his vehicle left something to be desired.

Such as proximity.

"Your car's parked in front of the precinct, remember?" Kelly prodded.

He frowned, which immediately told her that he *hadn't* remembered. The next moment, he shrugged. "Don't bother. I can call a cab."

Kelly was quick to veto the idea. "There's no need for you to spend the extra money. I take my responsibilities seriously."

Since when was he a responsibility? Especially hers? Kane waved away her words.

"That's okay—" he began.

"You turn me down and you'll hurt my feelings," she said out of the blue.

For a second, he stared at her, trying to decide

whether she was serious or just pulling his leg. He couldn't tell.

"What feelings?" he challenged. "If there was one thing I learned about you today, it's that you have the hide of a rhino."

Even if she had the face of an angel.

Kane immediately pulled back mentally as he simultaneously upbraided himself. Where the hell had that thought come from?

He supposed it was a clear indication that he *had* had too much to drink after all.

It irritated him beyond all reason that she was right.

Kelly seemed to take no offense at his comment. "Ah, yes, but under the tough outer layer beats a soft heart," she informed him. The corners of her mouth twitched a little as she did her best to keep her amusement from showing. "Okay, Durant, this is where we part company. See you in the morning."

She thought she heard him grunt something in reply just before he disappeared behind the door. The man's manners left something to be desired.

Kelly hurried back to her vehicle. She had barely pulled out of the spot when another car immediately swooped in, taking her place. There were few spots available at this time of night, she noted. Parking was at a premium. Not for the first time, she felt a wave of smug relief wash over her.

She'd made the right decision.

A little over a year ago she had given up apartment living and bought a small detached home. Among other things, this afforded her a driveway where she could always park her car. That in turn meant she no longer had to go searching for a parking spot at the most disadvantageous time of the evening.

Granted, a parking space had come with her previous apartment, but she'd lost count the number of times she'd come home, dead tired, only to find someone else had parked in her space. Like as not, the rental office would be closed for the night and she would have no recourse but to go trolling for an empty spot, not an easy feat at that time of night. Especially when all she really wanted to do was crawl into bed and get some well-deserved sleep.

She wouldn't have to go through that tonight. Not that she was even close to falling asleep this time. She had all manner of questions bouncing around in her head. They'd been bouncing around ever since she'd seen that odd look on Kane's face when she'd told him to think of her as family.

She needed answers and she had a feeling that asking Kane questions only would have made him clam up even more than he normally did.

The man could have auditioned to play a sphinx, she thought grudgingly, zipping through the yellow traffic lights.

The second Kelly let herself in the front door, she headed straight for the landline in the living room. At times the reception on her cell wasn't all that great and the signal cut in and out. She was in no mood to have interference get in her way.

Kelly paused only long enough to remove her service weapon and leave it within easy reach near the front door before she picked up the telephone receiver and started dialing.

The phone on the other end rang four times, then went to voice mail.

Valri wasn't home.

Swallowing an oath, Kelly debated hanging up and trying again at a later hour, but at best that would be hit and miss. If her younger sister, the best computer wizard she knew, came home sometime before midnight, she wanted Valri to call.

She wanted Valri to call even if it was *after* midnight, she decided.

Kelly said as much in the message she left.

"So call me," Kelly concluded. "I don't care what time you get in," she reiterated. "I need to talk to you, ASAP."

She blew out a breath and was just about to hang up the receiver when she heard the line on the other end being picked up.

"What's so urgent?" she heard Valri ask her. She sounded concerned.

"You're home," Kelly said happily.

"Apparently," Valri answered. "Now what's the emergency?"

"Why are you screening your calls?" Kelly asked.

There was a long pause and then she heard her younger sister say, "Could be because I'm doing something more important than talking to my sister."

That was an odd thing for Valri to say, Kelly thought. "What could be more impor—" And then it hit her. "Oh. You're not alone, are you?"

"And they said you weren't the bright one," Valri laughed.

It was obvious she wasn't about to identify who was with her—not that she really needed to.

"It's Alex, isn't it? He's the one with you," Kelly concluded, referring to her sister's fiancé.

Valri relented, giving up the pretense. "Two for two, not bad. Now, if you called just to shoot the breeze or complain about your new partner—"

"How do you know about my new partner?" Kelly asked, surprised.

"You forget, we Cavanaughs have our own special little network that spreads information faster than even the internet," Valri reminded her. "Okay, either talk fast, or I'll catch up with you tomorrow."

"I need some information on him," she said quickly. "My new partner. Kane Durant," she threw in for good measure, just in case Valri *didn't* know everything.

"So, ask him," Valri prodded.

"Ha!" Kelly dismissed that so-called option. "I'd

have better luck getting a statue to talk. Besides, I've got a feeling this is pretty personal."

"And you have the right to pry because…?" Valri asked.

"Don't get holier than thou on me, Valri," Kelly warned. "I need to know this so I don't accidentally say something to him that I'll wind up regretting." No way she wanted to trample on the man's feelings. Or accidentally unearth some deep, dark family secret.

"You *know* that's going to happen sooner or later no matter what kind of information I pass along to you. That kind of thing is just in your nature."

"Thanks for the vote of confidence," Kelly bit off. She wasn't about to give up until she had what she wanted. "Look, Val, I need to know about the man's family," she insisted. "It's important to me."

There was silence on the other end and Kelly knew she was getting to her sister.

"And you're sure he won't tell you if you ask nicely?" Valri asked.

"I'm sure. Trust me," Kelly answered. She stretched out on the sofa as she talked. "I told him that he should regard me as family and he got this really strange look on his face, like I'd just opened the door to something deep and dark. When I asked him if there were any girls in his family, he immediately changed the subject."

"Did you ever think that maybe he just didn't want

you to pry?" Valri asked her. "There are people like that, you know. People who don't want to give you their life history in the first ten minutes that they know you. Sometimes these things take time—like building up trust. That can't be rushed."

"There's more to it than that," Kelly insisted. "I can feel it."

"Well, why didn't you say so in the first place? Can't beat a scientific method like that," Valri quipped.

"Does Alex know what kind of smart mouth you have?" Kelly asked her.

"I'll have you know that Alex is very keen on my mouth, thank you very much." The next moment, Valri got down to business. "Okay, give me this guy's full name," Valri instructed with a resigned sigh. "I'll see what I can come through with."

"Thanks, Val. I knew you'd come around," Kelly said with enthusiasm and more than a little gratitude. "His name is Kane Durant. Detective, first class. I can hold on while you look him up," she volunteered.

"That's great, but you'll be listening to a dial tone eventually," Valri warned her. "The information I need to access is on the computer at work."

That didn't sound right to her. Valri could make a computer sit up, beg and roll over. This kind of thing should constitute a walk in the park for her.

"Since when has a little thing like proximity

stopped you?" Kelly asked. "Might I remind you that you're the one who hacked into—"

"Please, no trips down memory lane," Valri requested rather quickly, shutting down her sister.

Granted these were private lines they were on, but a little bit of paranoia was a healthy thing. It kept her, and the people who mattered, on their toes. The last thing Valri wanted was to have Kelly make a reference to her time as a successful hacker and possibly have that information go viral. Nothing good could possibly come of that.

"Besides," Valri went on, "that was then, this is now."

"Lovely title for a song," Kelly cracked. And then she sighed, relenting. "Okay, little sister. How long do I have to wait for the information?"

"Depends on how accessible it all is and how much I find," Valri told her. "I'll get started tomorrow morning. Good enough?"

"Guess it'll have to be."

"Why are you so curious about your partner's family, anyway?" Valri asked.

She was proud of hers, but not every family took its cues from Norman Rockwell's paintings. In some cases, family was the very last thing a person wanted to talk about.

Even if that person was a police officer.

"You wouldn't understand," she told Valri. Before her sister could mount some sort of a protest, she added, "You had to have been there."

"That's what people say when they don't want to go into detail about something," Valri told her.

"It's complicated," she said.

"Okay," Valri said, accepting her sister's answer since she had no other option. "Just as a side piece of information, how are you getting along with him?"

"I'm not sure yet," Kelly said honestly. "I'll let you know more once you get back to me about his family and I get to know him a little better—if that's possible." She laughed softly to herself, shaking her head. "I don't mind telling you that right about now I'm really missing Amos. With all of his strange quirks—needing to carry five coins in each of his pockets leaps to mind—the man was still an open book. This guy I want you to look into is more like a mystery—with all the pages glued together."

"Might be fun to unglue them," Valri told her. When Kelly sighed, her sister merely said, "I've seen what he looks like. Oh, and Brennan said the two of you were at Malone's earlier. You bought the drinks for you and this partner you're researching. That means you're bonding, right? He wouldn't have willingly gone with you if you weren't bonding."

"If by willingly you mean that I went after him, giving him no choice and then dragging him to the old ancestral stomping grounds here, then, yes, he came willingly."

"Unless the man is a ninety-pound weakling—and I know for a fact that he's not—you didn't drag Kane Durant anywhere that he didn't want to go. Some partnerships take time to establish," she reminded her sister. "You know that."

"Yeah, I know that," she agreed. But this was something that she just couldn't patiently stand around and wait for Kane to eventually reveal. She had a feeling that she needed to understand his background if this partnership between them was going to have a prayer of working. "Just get me as much of his background as you can, okay?"

"Shouldn't be that big a deal," Valri assured her. "I'll get back to you tomorrow morning. Fast enough for you?" she teased.

"It'll have to be," Kelly replied.

Valri sighed. "Good night, Kel."

"Good night," Kelly echoed. "And tell that good-looking guy next to you that I said hi."

"Maybe later," Valri replied in a very husky voice.

Kelly smiled wistfully to herself, envying Valri just a little as she hung up.

Chapter 8

A persistent, annoying buzzing scissored its way into her consciousness one jarring, pulsing disturbance at a time. It started out as a distant noise in the background, growing louder and louder until it felt as if the intruding sound was going to swallow her up.

Wrapping a pillow around her head, or at least managing to just barely cover her ears with it, didn't help to block out the noise. If anything, holding her pillow in that position woke her up instead of allowing her to drift back to sleep.

With a reluctant sigh of surrender, Kelly released her pillow and opened her eyes.

Darkness was still embracing the world, or at least it seemed that way in her bedroom. She was exhausted beyond words. It felt as if she'd just fallen asleep. Rolling over to her side, she looked at the blue digital numbers on her alarm clock.

Two a.m.

She *had* just fallen asleep, Kelly realized, feeling just the slightest bit justified for feeling lethargic.

But at least the buzzing had stopped. Had it been part of her dream or…?

The next moment, her question answered itself. The buzzing had started again.

It was her cell phone.

She glared at the culprit. Since this was obviously the second go-around, the odds of whoever on the other end of the call going away was slim to none.

Picking up her cell, she pressed Accept and mumbled a thick "Hello?" feeling more dead than alive right about then.

"We're up."

It took her a second to recognize the voice.

Durant.

Why would he be calling her in the middle of the night? Was this his clever way of getting even with her for some unknown transgression? Because her brain felt as if it had grown a layer of fuzz all over it, she couldn't connect the dots just yet.

But she would, Kelly silently promised herself. She would. And when she did, Durant was going to pay for this.

"No, we're not *up*," she responded. "You're talking in my sleep. Stop it."

"Would if I could, Cavanaugh. But we just caught another home invasion and, due to circumstances beyond my control, you're my ride, remember?"

The mention of another robbery, especially so soon after the first one, had Kelly sitting up and banishing all remnants of sleep from her brain.

"When?" she asked, kicking off her covers and getting out of bed as quickly as she could.

"As soon as you can get here," he told her.

"No, when did the home invasion happen?" she asked, clarifying her question.

Stumbling to her closet, she grabbed the first thing she could find. In this case, it was a pair of jeans and a sweater. The night air had a habit of getting chilly, with temperatures dropping by a full twenty degrees or more on occasion.

"Dispatch said the victim thought it was some time around eleven o'clock. It took the victims this long to untie themselves so they could call 9-1-1. How soon can you get here?" he asked.

"Fifteen minutes after I throw on some clothes," she told him, pulling fresh underwear out of her bureau drawer.

"You sleep naked?" It was meant to be a joke. He didn't expect the answer he received.

"Yes. Now the sooner we terminate this call, the sooner I can get to you." With that, she hit End and hurried into her undergarments and the jeans and sweater she pulled out of her closet.

Locating her shoes—she had a tendency to step out of them whenever the mood hit her, so they could be in any one of half a dozen places—took her a bit longer.

Dressed and ready in what still amounted to record time, Kelly spared one longing glance at her coffeemaker. The machine was programmed to brew at sixty-thirty and, consequently, was now standing silent and dormant.

Maybe Durant would have coffee ready, she thought.

Who was she kidding? Durant didn't strike her as someone who could sufficiently serve himself, much less someone else. And at any rate, it was highly doubtful he would be *that* thoughtful.

But at least it was something to hope for, Kelly told herself as she got into her car.

She dreamed about a large cup of coffee all the way to Kane's apartment.

"Quick enough for you?" she asked Kane twelve minutes later as he opened the door in response to her knock.

He hadn't expected her to show up *this* quickly. "How close to me do you live?" he asked.

"Let's just say I caught every light."

"Did you?" he asked, curious. He'd never managed to hit the trifecta when it came to quickly going from point A to point B.

"I said, let's just *say* I did," Kelly replied evasively. And then she saw what he had in his hands. "Are you planning on drinking both of those?" she asked, nodding at the two travel mugs he was holding.

"Forgot I was holding these," he confessed, somewhat embarrassed to come off so absentminded. "Here." He handed her one of the mugs. "I didn't know how you liked it so I didn't do anything to it. I've got milk and sugar in the kitchen if you need either."

She shook her head. "Thanks, but I think I need straight sludge to kick-start me this morning. Black is fine," she told him. Pausing to take a sip, she immediately shivered as the mouthful made its way down. "Okay, maybe I'll take you up on that milk and sugar," she said, changing her mind. She felt as if she'd just swallowed a mouthful of pitch.

"This way." He opened the door further to allow her to enter his apartment. The kitchen was right next to the front door. "Help yourself," he told her, gesturing toward the refrigerator.

Opening the refrigerator, she saw a small container of milk, a white carton she assumed had some sort of leftover take-out food in it and nothing else.

"Don't eat much, do you?" It was a rhetorical question.

She took out the milk carton and was just about to pour what little there was into her coffee, when her nose saved her.

After being assaulted by a pungent, stomach-turning smell, she quickly closed the carton again. What there was of the liquid was beyond spoiled. "I take it you're conducting a science experiment."

Kane appeared baffled. "What do you mean?"

"The milk smells positively rancid."

"No, it doesn't," he protested. But when he opened the spout to see for himself, he quickly changed his mind. "Yes, it does. Sorry about that," he added a tad apologetically.

"I'll settle for some sugar—as long as there aren't any tiny black bugs cavorting in it," Kelly qualified just in case.

Kane kept a small bowl of sugar in the center of the kitchen table. She approached it guardedly, then stirred in two spoonfuls of sugar. After tasting the results, she was satisfied that it was the best she could do.

She looked at her partner. "Okay, if you're ready, then let's go."

After following her out of the apartment, Kane locked the door behind him. He said nothing as he made his way to her car. Getting in, he buckled up and then focused on the travel mug in his hand.

When Kelly put her key into the ignition but didn't

turn it to start up the engine, he looked at her quizzically.

"I can't go until you tell me where we're going," she pointed out.

He banked down feeling stupid at the oversight. Instead, he immediately rectified it. "Twenty-two Coriander."

Kelly started the car, then slanted a glance at her partner. "If I hadn't asked for the address—let's say I'm psychic and the address just came to me—were you just going to sit there, silent, the whole trip?"

"Not that much of a trip," he told her matter-of-factly.

"The silence has a tendency to make it longer," she informed him.

He had kept quiet about this for as long as he could. The question seemed to all but erupt out of his mouth. "You really sleep naked?" he asked her. The image had been feeding on his brain since she'd inadvertently confirmed what he had so flippantly asked.

The question seemed to have come out of the blue. Suspicion entered the scene.

"Why?" Kelly asked. What difference did it make to know this piece of information about her?

Kane shrugged. "No particular reason," he told her with a degree of fabricated innocence. "I just thought you were pulling my leg. Were you?"

"You'll never know," she answered, smiling sweetly at him and content to leave him wondering rather than own up to what had become a habit for her. "Do you know any of the details about this home invasion we're going to be investigating?" she asked.

"Just that it sounds like the same guy breaking in. One person," Kane repeated almost grudgingly. It made her grateful that Kane wasn't after her.

More details lined up. The site of the second home invasion was a two-story house, located in the same general vicinity as the first house.

This time the thief had made off with a number of high-end electronics and some expensive jewelry. All in all, nothing about the invasion was remarkable, except that—again—the things the thief stole all had been located on the first floor and he could have gotten in and out without arousing any suspicions.

Despite that, the thief chose to wake the victims, tie them up, bring them downstairs and have them watch as he made off with their things.

"I suppose it's his form of bragging," Kelly commented.

"Something like that," Kane agreed.

"Was it just the couple present when he broke in?" she asked.

"According to the wife, they have kids, but the kids are away at school."

She squinted as she read the street sign, making sure she was headed in the right direction. "That's good. At least the kids weren't home at the time, being traumatized. That kind of thing could result in their being in therapy for years."

She rolled everything Kane had told her over in her head. "Maybe when we get back to the precinct we should double-check that these were isolated cases and that we haven't missed other home invasions that could be tied to this creep." A thought suddenly occurred to her. "Was there a security system?" If it was the same one, that would be their common denominator.

"Guess we'll find out, won't we?"

She smiled, reading between the lines. "Is that your clever way of saying you don't know?"

"That's my way of saying that dispatch only gave me a limited amount of information," he informed her rather abruptly. "And it serves no purpose to have you question me as if I was there when the home invasion was going down. I wasn't."

She nodded. "Good point. Want me to take you shopping when our shift is over?" she asked without any preamble or warning.

Kane stared at her. Where had that come from? "Why would I want to go to the mall with you?"

"Not *mall* shopping," she corrected. "Food shopping." There was a world of difference to the techniques employed in one versus the other. "And to answer your question as to why, it's because you have absolutely nothing edible in your refrigerator. You *do* eat, don't you?"

He thought back to the takeout he had sitting on the shelf. Granted he'd brought it home a few days ago, but it was still edible.

"Of course I eat. And as for not having anything edible in the refrigerator, that's just not true," he protested,

"Okay," she amended. "Nothing that won't land you in the emergency room having your stomach pumped," she told him. "How's that?"

He laughed shortly. There wasn't so much as a hint of a smile on his face. "I'll pass, thanks."

"You'll pass out," she corrected, "if you don't have anything edible at home."

He had to set her straight before she set up camp in his head.

"Look, Cavanaugh, for however long it lasts we're partners at work, we are *not*, I repeat *not*, 24/7 buddies. Just because we work together doesn't mean you can invade my private life like it's your God-given right."

"Actually, in a way it is," she pointed out. "It's in my best interest to keep you as healthy as possible. If you're not at the top of your game, how can you have my back?"

"Right now I'm getting visions of having your throat, not your back," he told her pointedly, leaving the rest unsaid. She struck him as bright enough to make all the necessary connections. "Were you like this with your last partner?" he asked.

"I didn't have to be," she said defensively. "Amos didn't believe in raising mold in his refrigerator. And he ate regularly"

Kane made a judgment call based on what he'd been observing. "I can see why the guy decided to bail out on you."

"He didn't bail out. He just felt like he was pushing his luck lately." Stopped at a red light, she looked at Kane and did a quick, obvious assessment. "You're grumpy," she noted. "If you had a good hot meal under your belt you wouldn't be grumpy."

He looked at her. A meal, hot or otherwise, wasn't going to negate the effect this woman had on those around her. Especially him. "I wouldn't bet on that if I were you."

Amused, Kelly laughed at the expression on Kane's face—among other things.

The sound annoyed him and seemed to seductively pull him in at the same time.

Maybe she was right, he thought grudgingly, although he'd die before admitting as much to her. But maybe these strange thoughts wouldn't be infiltrating his head if he'd taken something to eat with him.

There was always that drive-through place on the way back to the precinct, he reminded himself. He'd be able to get his breakfast there—provided the home invasion victims didn't talk his ears off.

Then again, he thought it was rather a safe bet that if *she* hadn't managed to accomplish that little feat yet, nothing the victims could tell him would be the least bit of a problem for him.

Just as with the first home invasion, a patrol car was parked outside the address Kane had given to her. The front door was wide-open to accommodate any necessary comings and goings involving the department.

She noticed that the CSI unit hadn't arrived on the scene yet.

"How long ago did you say that call came in to 9-1-1?" she asked Kane as she pulled up by the front curb.

"A little before 2:00 a.m. I called you the minute I got off the phone with dispatch," he added.

Not much time had elapsed between the call and their response time.

That would explain why the crime scene investigators hadn't arrived yet.

She nodded in response to what Kane had just told her. Bracing herself—in her opinion, it was never easy to face a victim of a crime—she said, "Let's see if the victims can enlighten us about the guy who robbed them."

Edward Mitchum was a tall, heavyset CEO of a local bank, and to say he was angry would have been a vast understatement. Pacing about his family room like a tiger in captivity searching for that one glimmer of freedom, Mitchum appeared to be building up steam. An amateur boxer in his younger years, Mitchum still looked capable of knocking out his opponent.

He also appeared none-too-pleased with the police in this case.

"That bastard better hope that you find him before I do." His booming voice resonated throughout the six-bedroom, six-bath house, only growing stronger as the minutes slipped by. "Because if I find him first, I'm going to wring his scrawny neck."

Kane suddenly looked alert. "Was it?"

"Was what it?" the man all but barked the question. He had been compromised and held captive, helpless to do anything to save himself or his wife, and it was obviously eating away at him.

"Scrawny. You just talked about the thief's scrawny neck. I'm just trying to verify whether or not you're using poetic license, or if you're actually describing accurately what you happened to witness," Kane explained.

Mitchum shrugged, obviously annoyed at the question as well as the situation he found himself in. He definitely wasn't accustomed to being on the receiving end of questions.

"I'm six foot one and two hundred pounds—"

"Two hundred and thirty," his wife interjected, speaking up for the first time.

"Nobody cares about the exact figure, Sienna,"

the CEO snapped. Turning back to the detectives, he continued. "To me, everybody looks scrawny."

"Point taken," Kane agreed. "You've got a lot of surveillance cameras planted throughout the house. Any chance that the man who broke into your house last night was caught on any of them?"

The woman shook her head. "None of the cameras were recording. He disconnected them," she explained. "He made a point of telling us that."

Unable to allow his wife to have the last word in any context, the bank president told them, "He spouted some technical garbage, saying he did this and that. Sounded really proud of himself."

"Please think this over," Kelly requested politely. "It's very important. Was he at all familiar to either of you?"

Mitchum scowled at her. "Are you saying you think it's someone we know? I'm a bank president. I don't associate with any lowlife."

"We didn't mean to imply that you did," Kelly assured him, attempting to soothe his ruffled feathers. "But maybe you encountered the man at one of the functions you attend on behalf of that foundation you started, donating meals to homeless shelters."

He'd done that strictly as a way of paying back some whimsical high priestess of luck who had somehow loaded the dice for him while standing in his corner. It seemed that no matter what he tried, he *always* managed to come out ahead.

Except this time.

Annoyed, the bank president began to wonder if he'd done something to break what had admittedly been a long-running lucky streak.

Superstition, he had come to learn, could exercise almost deadly control over people who found themselves on the wrong side of Lady Luck.

He intended to change that.

As soon as possible.

"No, he wasn't familiar to me," Mitchum swore.

Chapter 9

Edward Mitchum remained adamant about not knowing the man who broke into his house, referring to him as a "brazen, sadistic SOB." His irritation grew visibly at the very suggestion that someone within his sphere of acquaintances could have inflicted this act of humiliation on him.

After considerable resistance, he grudgingly agreed to draw up and send in a list of people with whom he interacted on a regular basis.

His wife, Sienna, had nothing to add. It was all she could do to keep from falling apart. The ordeal had clearly taken a huge toll on her.

Temporarily at a dead end, Kane told the couple they would be in touch and then he and Kelly left.

"Funny that both Mitchum and Osborn should have the same reaction for the experience they'd endured. Humiliation." Kelly rolled the word on her tongue, as if testing it out that way could help her piece together the disjointed evidence. She had a feeling that somewhere amid all this was the clue as to who had engineered these home invasions.

She slanted a look at Kane. His expression gave nothing away. The man was unreadable, and it frustrated her.

"I'm beginning to feel that there's a common thread running through these home invasions," Kelly said, getting into the car again. Her hands on the steering wheel, she looked at Kane again to see if any of this had started him thinking the same thing.

It hadn't.

"Which is?" Kane asked flatly. He was watching the road, his hands once more preemptively braced against the dashboard. It was obvious that he felt it was just a matter of seconds before a jolt vibrated through him.

"That our as-of-yet-unidentified suspect is robbing some pretty nasty people," she told him.

Kane laughed shortly. The sound was devoid of humor. "No argument there."

"Think that could be the unifying theme?" she asked, aware she was really reaching. "That someone is trying to get even with these people for some slight he'd endured at their hands?" As she spoke,

Kelly began to elaborate and expand on her fledgling theory. "Maybe the thief is actually some public servant or even a laborer that Osborn and Mitchum had both used at one time or another. And when they did, they behaved condescendingly toward him, so now he's getting even."

Kane wasn't convinced. "How do you explain the fact that the security system was disabled in both instances? A run-of-the-mill laborer isn't going to have that kind of knowledge or expertise."

She blew out a breath. "You can be a real downer when you want to be, Durant," she murmured. And then she relented. "But you're probably right. It was just a desperate shot in the dark," she admitted. "What's our next step, oh fearless leader?"

"We talk to some of the people who work for Mitchum. See if they can shed some light on this."

"Sounds like as good a place to begin as any," she agreed. Just then, the same kind of buzzing noise that had woken her up this morning resonated through her vehicle. She knew it couldn't be for her. "Either your pants are vibrating," she cheerfully said to Kane, "or that's your phone getting an incoming call."

Despite what she said, Kane made no move to pick up his smartphone.

Why wasn't he answering it? "Are you going to get that?" she asked. And then the reason for his reluctance suddenly occurred to her. He didn't want to talk in front of her. "I can pull over if you want privacy," she offered.

"Okay. Do that," he responded.

On his lips, it sounded more like an order and for a second, Kelly was tempted to tell him that she'd changed her mind about giving him privacy. But that would have been petulant and childish, so she refrained. She elected to take the high road first.

The moment she pulled her vehicle to a curb, Kane got out of the car. Whoever was on the other end of that call, Kelly mused, had to be very important to him.

Girlfriend?

Parent?

A hundred questions popped up and began multiplying in her head, especially while she watched Kane's back as he spoke to the person on his cell. Kane wasn't one to slouch—certainly he'd never done it around her—but he'd never stood at military attention before, either. He was now.

Something was up.

When he finally got off the cell phone and got back into her car, Kelly couldn't contain herself any longer. "Bad news?" she asked, paying close attention to his eyes, even though he deliberately avoided making eye contact.

"You might say that," he answered. He seemed preoccupied and more than a little upset. Someone on the other end of that call had gotten to him. But gotten to him how?

"Anything I can do to help?" she offered, hoping he would take her into his confidence even while she knew she hadn't a prayer of that happening.

Without realizing it, Kane sighed. "Not unless you have a time machine tucked away somewhere."

She thought of her brother, the one who actually believed there was more to science fiction than met the eye.

"Actually, that's something Malloy might be tinkering with."

"Malloy," Kane repeated, looking at her blankly. And then it hit him. "Another brother?"

She laughed, nodding. "You're getting good at keeping track of them, something even my own mother had trouble with from time to time." If she had a dime for each time her mother got their names confused, she would have been a very rich woman at this point in her life.

"What with seven kids—it is seven, right?" he asked her.

"Right." He did pay attention to details, she thought, surprised, and pleased—something that surprised her even more.

He continued, "With seven kids probably getting into trouble all the time, it's a wonder that your mother didn't lose her mind."

"She came close a number of times," Kelly told

him. Then her mind pivoted to a completely unrelated question. "Who was that call from?"

"Just some stranger," he answered evasively.

She didn't believe him. Even so, Kelly thought of just letting the subject go. But it really bothered her to be at this impasse with Kane. She was trying to build up a relationship so that he trusted her implicitly. When he behaved this way, it didn't exactly help build the kind of foundation needed to support a strong, trusting relationship.

"Did this stranger have a name?" she asked, keeping the subject open.

"Most people do," Kane answered drily.

Kelly ignored the sarcasm. Instead, she calmly asked, "Would you like to share that with the class or just hoard it like it's a big mystery?"

"It's personal," Kane informed her coldly.

His tone all but warned her not to trespass. For now, Kelly decided to back off. But not before saying, "You know you can talk to me about anything, right?"

"You mean whenever you're not talking?" he asked. "And since you're always talking, there's no way for anyone to get a word in edgewise, including me." It was clear he assumed that was the end of the discussion on this particular topic.

She wanted to protest what he'd just said, wanted to point out that she wasn't always talking, but she doubted it would do any good. It was obvious Durant had gotten an image of her in his head and he wasn't about to back off from it.

But she had to say *something*, had to go on the record protesting his image of her. "All you have to do is just say you want to tell me something important and I'll listen."

"I'll keep that in mind," he told her. But his mind was already elsewhere. The call he'd just taken had caught him completely by surprise. "Right now, I want you to head to the precinct."

She saw no reason for the side trip. "I thought we were interviewing the people who work with Mitchum at the bank."

"You're still doing that," he told her. "But I need my car. I've got something to do first. I need to take a couple of hours of personal time."

She'd almost gotten convinced that he didn't *have* a personal life. This shed an entirely different light on the man.

"You're sure I can't help in any way?" she asked again.

"All the help I need is to be dropped off at my car." It took an effort not to suck in his breath as she narrowly avoided colliding with another vehicle at the intersection. "Provided you don't kill us before we get to the precinct."

Several comebacks sprang to her lips, but she decided to keep them to herself, "I'll do my best not to."

* * *

"I'll be back as soon as I can," Kane told her when she dropped him off beside his sedan in the precinct parking lot ten minutes later.

She didn't get a chance to respond. Kane had slid behind the steering wheel of his car and sped off, going as fast, if not faster, than he had accused her of going just minutes ago.

Something was wrong, Kelly thought again. He wasn't a man who was agitated easily, yet he clearly had been when he'd taken off just now.

She intended to find out what had set him off if it was the last thing she did, she promised herself.

The interviews proved to be another dead end. Everyone she spoke to had polite words about Mitchum, but it was as if all interviewees had been reading from the same script.

Reading between the lines, she got the impression no one really cared for the bank president. Even so, she couldn't see any of the employees exacting revenge by breaking into Mitchum's home and terrorizing him as well as his wife before making off with electronics and jewelry.

Why electronics? Why not just jewelry or something more valuable? Granted the items that had been taken weren't cheap, but they wouldn't have fetched top dollar from a fence, either. Taking them was done for the purpose of embarrassing Mitchum, nothing more.

Since interviewing the people who worked at Mitchum's bank had proved to be unproductive, Kelly decided to talk to his neighbors. If she was lucky, one of them might have noticed something suspicious the evening of the home invasion.

It was a long shot at best, but for now, she was out of options.

Kelly was just about to begin questioning a third neighbor when Kane caught up to her.

The first thing she noticed was that he looked even more somber than usual. Somber and pale.

"Everything all right?" she asked. Judging by both his demeanor and his pallor, it wasn't. She fervently hoped the question could open up a dialogue between them.

He didn't answer her question.

Instead, he went right to the topic of the investigation. No surprise there. When it came to significant revelations Kane behaved as if he was the sphinx's direct descendant.

"Where did you get with the bank employees?" Kane asked.

"Far enough to know that the expression *Hear no evil, see no evil, speak no evil* is alive and well in some corners of this country—as well as at the Aurora First National Savings and Loan Bank."

Kane's eyes held hers for a long moment. "So you got nothing," he concluded.

It sounded so barren and final when he said it, she thought. But it was also true.

"I got nothing," Kelly confirmed. "I was just interviewing some of his neighbors, hoping that if maybe someone was fighting insomnia last night, they might have looked out their window and accidentally seen something that was out of place."

"Tall order," Kane commented.

She was well aware of that. But she also was aware that sometimes long shots paid off.

Her response was a tad defensive, but she wasn't about to make any apologies for it.

"Hey, if you get nothing by trolling, you start thinking of climbing out on a limb and hopefully, getting lucky."

"And this is you, out on a limb?" he asked.

She couldn't tell if he was asking a legitimate question or being sarcastic. In any event, she only had one answer for him. "Metaphorically speaking."

"Okay, let's see if we can 'get lucky.'" He paused before adding, "Metaphorically."

She was more than happy to oblige.

The same general feeling that had surfaced when she had questioned the bank employees was echoed by Mitchum's neighbors. It was also obvious, once the politely worded rhetoric had been scrubbed and set aside, that none of the neighbors really knew either the bank president or his wife. The couple kept to themselves.

The last neighbor they spoke with, a divorcée named Arlene Richards, found the Mitchums lacking in several areas. She wasn't shy about listing what she viewed as shortcomings, either.

"And they never participate in anything that the association plans."

"The association?" Kelly asked, exchanging looks with Kane.

"The Home Owners Association," Arlene Richards explained. "We've held block parties as well as fund-raisers for the local animal shelter. Couldn't get either of them to donate their time or part with a dime." She frowned, a note of disgust evident in her voice. "I guess Mr. Mitchum has found a way to take it with him. Please don't tell him I said so," she suddenly requested when she realized what she had said.

"Your secret's safe with us," Kane assured the woman.

Aside from wearing a dress that could have doubled as a full body tourniquet, Arlene was doing her best to flirt with Durant. He, on the other hand, seemed totally oblivious to the woman's attempts, as well as her very obvious "charms."

The first chance she got, Kelly promised herself she was going to call Valri and see how far her sister had gotten with putting together a bio on Durant.

Ordinarily, she would have conducted her own investigation, but she knew without asking that getting firsthand information out of Durant would be next to impossible. And if she made any calculated guesses, she had a feeling Durant would just deny everything or clam up, neither of which would be remotely satisfying.

Kelly noticed that this time around her partner did *not* hand the older woman his card and urge her to call if she thought of anything pertinent to the case.

"Did you forget to give her your card?" she asked innocently once they'd left the woman's estate.

"I didn't forget," Kane answered in a dismissive tone.

"Smart move," Kelly told him.

Kane grunted something unintelligible in response. Kelly wisely kept a straight face.

Temporarily at an impasse, they decided to go back to the precinct to review what they knew about the two cases. Kelly was hoping something would occur to them that had been overlooked, although she wasn't holding out too much hope at the moment.

When the facts were listed beneath each pair of home invasion victims, the only similarity found was that the couples both resided in the more affluent part of the city. Beyond that, their paths didn't appear to cross. They didn't frequent the same restaurants, didn't belong to the same organizations and they didn't donate to the same charities. They didn't even bring their vehicles to the same mechanic to be serviced.

"Maybe whoever's doing this just hates rich people," Kelly suggested.

"You said something earlier about seeing if there were any other recent home invasions either here or in one of the neighboring cities. Have you done that yet?" Kane asked.

"Not yet," she answered. Her fingers were already on the keyboard. "But I'll get right on it."

"Might as well since we don't exactly have a hot trail to follow," he commented. Kane was about to say something further to her on the subject, but his cell began to chime. "I've got to take this," he told her without bothering to look at the caller ID. He stepped out into the hall.

Her curiosity instantly activated, Kelly was sorely tempted to follow him into the hall and eavesdrop. Granted that wouldn't be a way to build up trust, but it could give her some answers.

With her search engine going through the database she had tapped into, Kelly took the opportunity to call her sister.

The second she heard Valri pick up on the other end and say "Hello?" Kelly immediately lowered her voice and asked, "Did you find out anything about Durant yet?"

"Kelly?"

"Of course it's me." Kelly lowered her voice even

further. "Did anyone else ask you to look Durant up?" she asked Valri.

"Point taken. Sorry," Valri apologized. "It's been one of those days from hell. To be honest, I've just now managed to pull up the information you asked about."

Kelly was instantly alert. "What did you find out?" she asked eagerly.

Valri paused as if she was reading something. "Well, he's gone through a large number of partners."

Kelly struggled to contain her impatience. "I already know that, Val," she told her sister. "Is there anything else?"

"Hold it. I see something noted down here." There was another pause, far shorter than the first one. "Oh my God."

"What?" Kelly cried. It was obvious that whatever Valri was reading had caught her off guard. "Talk to me. What did you find?"

Valri let out a shaky breath. "There was a lot of domestic abuse when Durant was growing up."

It wasn't all that uncommon. There had to be something more to it if it had disturbed Valri to this extent.

"How bad?" Kelly asked.

"Bad. Really bad," Valri emphasized. "His father shot his mother right in front of him when he was ten years old."

That explained a lot of things, Kelly thought, especially Kane's distant attitude. "Did he kill her?"

"Yes," Valri answered grimly. "But that's not all. It says here in the report that Kane tried to protect his mother, so his father shot him, too, and then he killed himself."

"Murder-suicide," Kelly stated grimly.

"That's what it looks like," Valri agreed. There was a hitch in her throat. "Doctors said it was a miracle that Kane survived."

"With that in his background, no wonder he's not exactly bright and cheery. Given the circumstances, someone else might have turned around and become a serial killer," Kelly said, shaking her head. "Was Durant placed into foster care after they released him from the hospital?"

"No. It says here that his uncle took him in." There was another pause as Valri continued reading. "His uncle was a cop until he retired from the force."

"Anything else?" Kelly asked, praying there wasn't. Durant's life sounded positively Dickensian. No wonder he was so grim most of the time. Hard to smile with that kind of thing in his background.

"Not that I can see. I'll do a little more digging when I get a chance," Valri promised. "But I've got to go now."

"Thanks, Val, I appreciate it," Kelly said, terminating the call.

She had just put away her cell phone when she

saw Kane entering the squad room. He was dragging his hand through his dark blond hair and he
looked agitated.

She waited for him to return to his desk and
asked, "Is everything okay?"

"You keeping tabs on me, Cavanaugh?" Kane
snapped, a storm gathering in his intense blue eyes
as he sat down.

The last thing he would accept was pity. She knew
that, so she proceeded accordingly. "Just being concerned," she answered, tossing her head. "No need
to take my head off."

He leaned back in his chair, dragged a hand
through his hair. "Sorry, it's been kind of a rough
morning and I've got a lot on my mind."

Kelly thought of what her sister had just told her.
Despite her promise to herself about keeping her distance and not invading his space, her heart just went
out to him. He looked as if he was in pain and her
inclination was to try to lessen that pain.

"They say sharing makes the burden lessen,"
Kelly told him.

"And where is it that they say these things? How
do you make sense out of something that just defies
logic?" he demanded.

When Kane saw that several sets of eyes had
turned toward them, his frown only deepened and
he turned his chair away from their line of vision.

Kelly pulled her own chair all the way in and

leaned forward, keeping her voice low. "Okay, I think it's time you told me what's bothering you."

His emotional state felt raw and vulnerable. Kane snapped at her. "And I think it's time for you to back off, unless you want to find yourself being partnered up with someone else by the end of the day.

"In fact, why don't you start filling out those papers you have to file to get a new partner? This just isn't working," he told her.

Oh, no. You don't get rid of me that easily.

"No," she said, surprising him. "I don't want another partner. I can't just abandon you when you're obviously dealing with something, even if you *are* a giant pain in the butt. Someone has to stick by you. It might as well be me."

Rather than answer her, Kane got up from his chair and strode out of the squad room.

Chapter 10

Less than half a minute later Kelly was on her feet, hurrying to catch up to her noncommunicative partner. She overtook her quarry, who was heading down the hallway, in a matter of seconds.

"Where are you going?" she asked once she'd caught up to Kane.

"I don't know," he retorted. "Anywhere that you're not."

The blunt answer did not cause her to retreat. On the contrary, she dug in. "I'm not the problem," she informed Kane.

"Wanna bet?" the detective challenged.

She blew out a breath. "Okay, you don't want me

asking questions, I won't ask questions. Let's just focus on the home invasions," she proposed.

He gave her a dark look.

Durant appeared as if he could shoot lightning bolts at her if he wanted to, she thought.

"Trying to lull me into a false sense of security, is that it?"

"I'm trying to earn my pay," Kelly told him flatly. "Now stop going all Harry Callahan on me and come back to the squad room. I've got something to show you." She began to walk back to the room they had just vacated.

Kane didn't. He remained exactly where he was. "Harry who?" he asked, sounding both bewildered and suspicious.

"Callahan," she repeated. She couldn't believe her partner wasn't aware of the cult classic movie. "The police detective Clint Eastwood played in *Dirty Harry*. The guy who single-handedly cleaned up the streets of San Francisco." With each added piece of information about the movie, she kept looking at Kane to see if she'd gotten him to remember. The expression on the other detective's face told her she'd struck out. "Well, at any rate, he wasn't exactly the easiest guy to be around, either," Kelly concluded.

Because he was on the clock and the case remained opened, Kane had no choice in the matter. He began to walk back to the squad room.

"Did this Harry guy have a partner like you?" he asked.

"No, he wasn't that lucky," Kelly said.

Her answer was met with a laugh. "That's not the word I'd use," Kane told her. "So what is it you want to show me?" he asked.

Kelly pointed to her desk. Specifically to the computer monitor.

"Following up on our discussion, I found two prior home invasions. One took place a little more than two weeks ago in Sacramento. The other one occurred last week in Merced." Sitting down at her desk, she pointed to each home invasion on the monitor. "The MO is identical to the robberies that took place here in Aurora."

"Instead of a week between invasions, these last two robberies were just a day apart," Kane pointed out, more to himself than to her. "Looks like our thief has stepped up his program. Wonder why."

"Could be as simple as the proximity," Kelly guessed. "The first two were spread out. The last two were in the same city. Hell, they were practically in the same neighborhood."

Kane nodded. And then he looked at her. "Want to go interview the first two victims?" It was more of a suggestion than a question.

He was rewarded with a wide grin. The grin transformed an already very pretty face into an utterly compelling one.

The fact that he noticed it at all bothered Kane. He wasn't supposed to think of his pain-of-a-partner as anything but a fellow detective. Seeing her as a *female* detective was bad enough. Seeing her as an *attractive* female detective was far worse.

Moreover, for some reason that awareness infiltrated his subconscious and sorely interfered with his ability to concentrate, much less be able to cleanly process a thought.

"I thought you'd never ask," Kelly responded to his suggestion.

It struck him as a little too enthusiastic. Yet, just as he found her, he found her go-get-'em trait exceedingly attractive.

Kane upbraided himself. He usually maintained better control over his thoughts than this. *This* was really beginning to concern him.

He needed to work. To keep busy and not think about anything other than the case. Not just because of the very obvious reason that had come up, but because of his general reaction to this woman, as well. She was starting to occupy more and more of his mind, not just when he was with her, but when they weren't together.

That had to come to an end immediately.

"Take down their addresses and let's go," he told Kelly gruffly.

When they walked out to the parking lot behind the building, he saw Kelly walk purposely toward the left lot. That wasn't where the woman had last parked, he remembered.

"Where are you going?" Kane asked.

"To your car," she answered. She saw the quizzical, albeit unvoiced, question in his eyes and answered that, as well. "I just figured that since your car was accessible, you'd want to drive."

"And you're not challenging that?" he asked, surprised. He had her pegged as a control freak. Was he wrong?

"You're the lead on this," she replied mildly. "It's your right to make the final decisions regarding everything about the case, including who drives what as well as where," Kelly told him calmly.

"I'm impressed. You actually managed to say all that with a straight face," he observed, opening the driver's side door.

The other locks were released. Kelly opened the door on her side of the vehicle. "Why wouldn't I?" she asked him innocently. "The captain made you the lead, didn't he?"

That was beside the point, or so he had thought. "I really didn't think you let little things like that get in your way."

She looked at him as he started up the car. The engine all but purred in response.

"My way?" she questioned.

"Your way," he repeated, then illustrated what he meant. "You just plow straight through until you've done whatever it is that you think needs to be done. And even then you don't retreat. You stand guard, making sure no one else messes with your project."

She had a strong hunch that her "plowing" days were behind her now.

Kelly shrugged. "Being partnered with someone means having to make certain adjustments. The bottom line is to solve the cases and make sure that the crime rate is contained at an acceptable number."

"When it comes to crime, there is *no* acceptable number," he informed her.

"In an ideal world," she agreed readily. Then she reminded him, "But this isn't an ideal world we're dealing with."

The very thought had Kane laughing. Kelly felt as if she and her partner had somehow changed their basic beliefs. Without fully realizing it, she had become the realist while Kane had somehow turned into what passed for an idealist.

The latter was obviously having the same thought. "If I didn't know any better, I'd say that I was having a nightmare."

His interpretation surprised her. "What makes you say that?"

"Because this is one hell of a role reversal for us," he told her.

"Maybe you just always wanted to be an idealist, and since I really can't honestly be one, you jumped right in to fill the position."

"How come you can't be an idealist?" Given her personality he really found that hard to believe.

"With my entire family involved in law enforcement, and a large number of them serving right here in Aurora, I am acutely aware of the fact that conditions out in the real world aren't exactly ideal—no matter how much I wish they were."

He still didn't think that made actual sense, but for the time being he refrained from pointing that out. "For the record, nobody could ever accuse me of being an idealist," he told Kelly.

"Maybe a closet idealist," she suggested.

Again he laughed, the sound so dry it was almost physically irritating. "Not in a closet, not even in a cave," he told her with finality.

Raising her hands in surrender, Kelly backed off. "Okay," she told him. "I stand corrected. You're *not* an idealist. Never were. Never will be. How's that?"

She noticed that didn't seem to satisfy him. He was frowning. What he said next didn't seem like a fitting reason for him to look the way he did.

"You're being amicable," he told her.

Why did he sound so annoyed when he made that observation? Most people would have appreciated the gesture—and the effort it involved.

"I'm trying," she answered.

"Well, stop it," he ordered, completely surprising her. "It's like waiting for an ax to fall," he told her. "And the suspense will wind up killing me."

A normal person would have applauded the effort, she thought, not found something negative about it.

"You're making it very hard to get along with you. You do realize that, don't you?" she asked.

"Then stop trying to get along with me," he retorted dismissively.

"Do you *want* people not to like you?" she asked.

He shrugged. "I really don't care one way or the other."

Stunned, Kelly glared at her cantankerous partner for a long moment before loudly declaring, "Bull!"

"What did you just say?"

She gladly repeated it for him. "I said bull. If you didn't hear that, then you're deaf as well as thickheaded—not to mention terminally stubborn." She wasn't finished yet. "And I'm not buying into the act."

Judging from his profile, his scowl had deepened by several degrees. "I don't know what you're talking about. There is no act," he informed her with finality.

She still didn't believe him. "If you honestly think that, then you've managed to fool yourself. But you haven't fooled me." Before he could contest what she had asserted, Kelly gave him her reasons for believing as she did. "No one is as indifferent to what people think and feel about them as you pretend to be. Like it or not, on some level people care about what other people think about them. Even you."

He snorted, showing his contempt for her theory. "No, I don't."

"Then you'd be the first," she told him. "Even serial killers care. If they didn't, they wouldn't be doing things that would net them the kind of attention that they get," she pointed out. "And good or bad, they view attention to be a way of validating their existence."

"With all this so-called insight you seem to have into people, why did you become a cop? Why didn't you become a psychiatrist?" Kane said sarcastically.

Kelly didn't have to think about her answer. "Too much sitting involved. I'd wind up spreading out. Besides, I like taking an active part in life, not sitting on the sidelines, commenting on it."

If she felt that way about it, then why was she dispensing all this so-called insight into his psyche? "And yet, here you are, commenting on mine. You're contradicting yourself, Cavanaugh."

"No, I'm not," she maintained. "In this case it's called trying to help."

"It's called meddling," he said.

She expected no less from him. He was fighting dirty, but he also seemed to be fighting for what was left of his professional life.

"Potato, po-tah-to," Kelly countered.

"You got anyone special in your life?" he asked.

Coming out of nowhere, the question almost threw

her. It took her a moment to summon her composure. "Everyone's special in my life."

He stared at her. "Are you trying to get me to up-chuck right here?" he asked.

"I'm just answering your question," she said, pretending innocence. But then her curiosity got the better of her. "Why are you asking me if I have someone special in my life?"

"Because if you did I was going to send him the best bottle of scotch money could buy—along with my condolences."

"Well, you can save your money and your condolences," she told him. "Because there is nobody."

He had to admit that sounded a little hard to believe, not because she was so damn pretty, but because she was part of the Cavanaugh family.

"How come?" he asked. "Aren't you Cavanaughs supposed to be nesters?"

She had a sudden image of birds flocking around, searching for a place to land and homestead. It almost made her laugh.

"When the right person comes along to make that nest with, then, yes, we're nesters," she allowed. "Unfortunately, nobody ever came around who measured up to my standards."

"Big surprise there," Kane murmured under his breath. "You have any particulars on the first home invasion victim?" he asked, deciding to completely change the subject.

The discussion they'd been having was getting far too heated for his comfort despite the seemingly pointed verbal exchange. And, despite his best efforts to the contrary, Kane could feel himself getting stirred up in a way that completely disquieted him.

The matter, he felt, was best dropped and left alone.

He watched as Kelly checked with the notes she'd transferred to her smartphone.

"Only that he lives alone, is considered a real catch according to some exclusive, snobbish magazine, and the night of his home invasion, Daniel Wilcox was entertaining—as he seems to do a good many school nights. Wilcox and the lucky lady who was his choice for the evening had both been asleep—as usual—when the invasion took place. They were dragged out of bed at gunpoint, tied up with the same kind of twist ties that were used on the two couples in Aurora, and the thief seemed to take extra pleasure in humiliating Wilcox in front of his so-called girlfriend or whatever she was supposed to be."

Kane was listening to her and processing his own thoughts on the matter at the same time. And then he sat up straighter as a stray observation suddenly occurred to him.

"How old is Wilcox?" he asked Kelly.

She paused for a moment, looking that information up in her notes. "Thirty-eight. Why?"

Kane didn't answer her, but asked her another question. "How old were the first home invasion victims in Aurora?"

"In their later thirties. So was the second couple," she told him before he could ask. "You think that's the connection? Their similar ages?" she questioned incredulously.

"What I'm thinking," Kane said, going a step further than dwelling on the age, "is that they might all know each other. Or at least that they *did* know one another at one point."

"So we're back to the idea that our thief is after some kind of revenge instead of actually just doing this for monetary gain?" She liked the former rather than the latter.

"I think that it's a distinct possibility," he told her.

She saw no reason to quibble with that. Durant very well could be right. "I'll get someone in the squad to take a picture of the photographs we've got on the bulletin board so we can show them to the first victim."

And maybe, just maybe, she added silently, they could finally get somewhere.

Daniel Wilcox, a thrice married and divorced multibillionaire—the latter thanks to his late father's investment efforts—looked far from happy to be interviewed by police detectives from another city about what he freely told them was "the worst possible night of my life."

"Look, as far as I'm concerned the whole damn experience is all behind me—and I want it to stay there." He gestured around what could only be termed as a mansion. "I've had a brand-new, state-of-the-art security system put in and, in addition, I've hired a bodyguard." With a studied shrug, he dismissed the incident that had happened to him previously.

"These things happen, but I've taken the proper precautions to keep it from ever happening again." Obviously to Wilcox that was the end of it. Kelly almost felt sorry for the man's incredible naïveté.

"I don't see what more I can tell you that I didn't already tell the detectives who originally came out to take my statement," Wilcox said impatiently.

"Well, for starters, could you please just take a look at these two photographs?" Kelly requested, holding up her cell phone directly in his line of vision. She slowly went from one couple's photograph to the other. "Do you recognize either one of these couples?"

Kelly went on to recite all four of the victims' names, including the women's maiden names. She thought she saw a glimmer of recognition in the man's face, but the next moment it was gone and he shook his head.

"No, sorry, don't recognize any of them." With

an innocent look that was almost *too* innocent, Wilcox asked, "Why?"

"We were hoping there was some sort of a connection. They were all victims of home invasions similar to the one that you were forced to go through," Kane told him.

"You people better up your game, then," was the victim's comment. "Now, if there's nothing further, I have a young lady waiting to receive the pleasure of my company." He turned to a tall, beefy man who was never more than a heartbeat away. "Show these people out, Ryan," he instructed the bodyguard.

"That's all right. We can show ourselves out," Kane assured the hulking man. "We know the way," he added for good measure.

In what amounted to a protective gesture, Kane put his hand lightly on the small of his partner's back and guided her to the front door.

The contact surprised her. The fact that she felt her stomach muscles tighten ever so slightly, as well as her pulse quicken, surprised her even more.

For a second she completely forgot about the uncooperative robbery victim and his paid shadow.

Chapter 11

"Well, that turned out to be a colossal waste of time," Kane bit off once they had walked out of Daniel Wilcox's palatial house. Kane continued to keep his hand against her back until they reached his sedan.

The case, think about the case, not the fact that Durant's hand feels so right against your back, idiot, Kelly kept telling herself.

It didn't really help.

"Maybe not," she told her partner, doing her best to focus on what he was saying and not what he was doing.

Dropping his hand, Kane was instantly alert. "Did he say something to you?" he asked.

How had he missed an exchange between the two, he wondered. Wilcox hadn't been out of his sight the entire time.

"Not in so many words—" Kelly began.

Okay, false alarm, Kane thought darkly. "Did he say something to you in *any* words?" he asked.

Kelly got into the car and buckled up. "There was a look of recognition on his face. Just for a second," she qualified.

"Oh. A *look*. Great." He made no effort to hide his sarcasm.

She ignored the dismissive note in Kane's voice. "I just think that he knows more than he's saying."

"It would be hard for him to know less. We could take him in for questioning, but if he doesn't want to talk, he doesn't want to talk," Kane emphasized. "And when you get down to it, the guy's a victim, not the guilty party."

"I know, I know," Kelly answered, frustration pulsing in her voice. "But this does fit in with your idea that whoever's conducting these home invasions knows his victims and is robbing them of their most prized possessions out of some sense of revenge, not because he's out for the money."

Though it was his theory, he was still on the edge about it. However, there were procedures to follow.

"Maybe we need to dig deeper. See if these victims belong to the same health clubs, church, took a vacation together, frequent the same restaurant, invested in the same stocks—anything that would connect them in any way possible."

She nodded. It would be tedious, but perhaps fruitful.

"Are we going to talk to the other victim now?" she asked. It was getting kind of late in her estimation, but since Durant was the lead on this case, he had to make the call.

Kane glanced at his watch, then shook his head. There was some place he wanted to be and it didn't involve questioning another victim who most likely would have no useful information to give them.

"It's late," he told her. "We can drive back up tomorrow."

Kelly studied her partner for a long moment. Something in his voice told her he wasn't as focused as he normally was.

"You have somewhere to be?" she asked, seemingly casual. In reality, she was anything but.

"Why?" he asked suspiciously.

"You've looked at your watch a few times in the last couple of hours. That's not like you," she observed. "You usually don't seem to care what time it is."

"We haven't been working together long enough for you to use the word *usually*," he told her. "Maybe I just don't want to wear you out." His tone was flippant.

"Like I believe that," she scoffed. "Just how dumb

do you think I am?" she challenged. "And before you answer that, consider the question carefully."

"With an army of relatives at your disposal, I wouldn't think of touching that comment with a ten-foot pole."

She tried not to take offense, but she wanted to make sure he understood how she operated. "I fight my own battles, Durant. If you pick a fight with me, me is all you're going to get."

To her surprise, Kane smiled, apparently amused by what she had just said. "I guess that's more than enough."

"You'd better believe it." Kelly paused for a moment, debating whether to put herself out there and deciding she had nothing to lose. Overtures of friendship ultimately never were wasted. Sometimes it just took more than a single effort. "You want to stop for dinner?" she asked him.

She saw the detective glance at the digital clock on the sedan's dashboard. "Can't," he told her.

"Can't? Or won't?"

"Can't," he repeated. "And before you say anything, I do know the difference," he emphasized, shooting her a pointed look.

"Okay. Is there anything I can help with?" she volunteered. The only way she would get any real answers from Durant was if she could crack that no-trespassing exterior of his and find out just what was going on inside.

"You could check that database again to see if there were any more home invasions that fit our thief's MO. The more people we question, the more likely that *something* is going to come to light that ties these invasions together."

"Consider it done," she assured him. "Don't forget it could still be just what you said earlier—a matter of some maniac with a grudge against people who don't live from paycheck to paycheck."

"I know," he replied. She didn't need to remind him of his own idea. "But I can't shake the feeling that it's really something more," he added, then shrugged. "I could just be shadowboxing in the dark."

"Then that makes two of us," she told him. "Because I've got the same feeling after I saw that look on Wilcox's face."

As Kane drove them back to Aurora, twilight began to tiptoe in, cloaking the road ahead in murky darkness.

Kelly chewed on her lower lip, debating whether to prod her partner about his evasiveness. She couldn't shake the feeling that something was bugging him and it really bothered her, more than she wanted to admit. Asking him about it wouldn't get her anywhere, but maybe, if she offered him some sort of a diversion, eventually he might share just a little of what was on his mind.

"What are you doing this weekend?" she asked, the question coming out of the blue.

"Why would you want to know?"

The man never merely volunteered information. Everything turned into a chess game with him.

Kelly told herself just to jump in rather than go through the trouble of feeling the man out before she spoke. "I thought you might want to have a really good meal, that's all."

"You're offering to cook?" he asked a little uncertainly.

He wasn't prepared to hear her laugh. Nor was he prepared for the effect that sound had on him. Her laughter was infectious and, though the fact made him far from happy, he found it rather irresistible.

"I'd be offering to poison you if I did that," Kelly told him quite honestly. "No, Andrew is holding one of his famous brunches, and I thought that maybe you'd like to come over and enjoy a good meal and some good company to boot."

"What makes you think I need either?"

"Well, most people don't turn down a good meal—unless they're pretentious gourmets—and only hermits turn down good company."

There was no point in pretending he could cook. He couldn't, not beyond basic survival mode, which involved scrambled eggs and toast. But he could lay claim to the latter if need be.

"Maybe I am a hermit," he countered.

Kelly didn't bother pretending she was considering that.

"No, if you were a hermit, you wouldn't be involved in a line of work that has protect and *serve* as its credo.'" She studied him again. There was nothing but the open road and time in front of them, so she decided to risk asking. "Why *did* you become a cop, anyway?"

He thought of telling her that it was none of her business, but that seemed rather a harsh response in light of the concerned way she'd been acting. The woman was getting more and more difficult to just push away.

So he told her the truth, thinking that in this instance she wouldn't be able to make any connections. "Somebody I admired was a cop. I thought I could do worse than follow in his footsteps."

That would be his uncle, the man who ultimately had taken him in and raised him after he'd suffered the worst kind of tragedy that could befall a child.

She almost blurted out as much, but then Kelly remembered she wasn't supposed to know about his uncle or the rest of his background. She wasn't good at lying or at containing her responses. But she knew she had to make some sort of effort.

Kelly decided to try a different approach to get her partner to lower his guard and allow her in, at least partially.

Baby steps, she cautioned herself. "Can I ask you who that was?" Kelly watched his profile as he drove.

Kane never even flinched. "You can ask," he told her.

Kelly could read easily between the lines.

"But you're not going to tell me," she guessed.

She saw the corner of his mouth rise just a little. She'd guessed right. Just then his single word of victory confirmed her thoughts.

"Bingo," he said.

She decided to leave the matter alone. At least for now. If she pushed too hard she would negate everything she'd managed to accomplish until now.

"Okay, you're entitled to your secrets," she told him.

Her answer aroused his curiosity.

"What are you up to?" he asked, eyeing her suspiciously.

"Nothing," she told Kane in all innocence. Then she stated firmly with a wide grin, "But you are coming to brunch."

"I don't think so," he answered with finality. As far as he was concerned, there was no *think* about it. He had no intention of attending anything that had any social implications whatsoever.

"Afraid?" she challenged slyly.

From her vantage point she could see his eyes. They had suddenly grown steely. "Not interested," he told her in a monotone voice.

"Everyone's interested in eating," Kelly informed her partner. "Besides, some of the people who will be there are people you interact with."

And she thought that was a selling feature? Kane found himself wondering.

"My point exactly," he told her. "I see them on the job. There's no reason for me to have to see them after hours."

He was putting up more of a fight than a freshly caught marlin. Two could play that game, Kelly thought.

"Okay, how about this?" she said gamely. "You attend the brunch and I'll do all the reports for both of us for the next week—"

"No," Kane answered flatly.

"For the next *two* weeks," she countered.

His answer remained the same and he delivered it without so much as glancing her way.

"No."

"Okay." This was her final offer. After this, she didn't intend to keep going. She'd find another way to bring the antisocial Kane to the table. "A month. I'll do all the arrest reports for a full month." She watched his face as she made the offer. It remained impassive. "C'mon, Durant. You *hate* writing reports."

Kane kept up his guard. He'd gone his whole life this way, but the heavy veneer was beginning to crack. "How would you know that?"

"Because *everyone* hates writing reports."

He raised one inquisitive eyebrow. "That means you do, too."

"Guilty as charged, your honor," she replied with an exaggerated nod of her head.

"But you're willing to do them for a month to get me to come to some brunch?"

"Not just *some* brunch. One presided over by the legendary Andrew Cavanaugh. But to answer your question, yes," she repeated. "I'm willing to do them for a month if you come to the brunch."

Picking up speed on what was close to a deserted stretch of freeway, Kane repeated the same question. "Why?"

She placed no spin on it, feeling honesty was what ultimately would sell this to her partner.

"Because I think you need it. Because this lone-wolf thing of yours is getting old. Because there isn't a single human being who doesn't respond to the kind of warmth that a good family provides. And that includes you," she concluded, giving him a very steely eye in the bargain.

Kane was struggling to keep his irritation in check. "Look, Cavanaugh, I appreciate what you think you're trying to do—"

She cut him off, not wanting to ruin the sentiment. "Good, then you'll come," she said as if it was a done deal.

Kane sighed wearily. "You're not going to give

me any peace about this latest thing of yours until I say yes, is that it?"

Her smile all but raised the temperature in the car. "That's it."

She was getting to him—and he really couldn't have that, he thought darkly. He couldn't become a lighter, warmer version of himself. Nice guys didn't finish last. They got creamed before the credits even rolled on the screen.

"Then I guess I'm going to have to ask for another partner in order to make it—and you—stop."

Kelly brazened it out. "It's not going to work, you know," she informed him. "HR is not going to let you have another partner." Mentally, she crossed her fingers and hoped that in the wider scheme of things, she would be forgiven for the lie. "You have a choice of sticking it out with me or getting placed on administrative leave

"So, when you stack that up against just agreeing to attend an informal breakfast with a great bunch of people for a couple of hours, it doesn't really seem like that big a deal," she told him.

It was obvious he was stuck going to this brunch. He didn't like not having control over a situation, no matter how minor.

His eyes narrowed as he threw her a glance. "You're my own personal plague, aren't you?"

She offered him a beatific smile. "I'd rather think of myself as your personal guardian angel."

"No," he contradicted. "Plague. I got it right to begin with." Kane blew out a long breath. She never took her eyes off him as he wrestled with the problem, debating in silence. "All right," he surrendered. "I'll come. Just this once, I'll come. But after that, you have to leave me alone about this kind of thing or suffer the consequences."

"Consequences?" Kelly questioned, more curious than worried.

He wasn't about to be won over. Certainly not so quickly. "Trust me, you won't want to know."

"But you will come, then?" she questioned. The more securely she pinned him down, the better the odds were of his actually showing up.

He nodded. "Just give me the time and place."

"I'll do better than that," she assured him. "I'll come and pick you up."

He quickly vetoed the idea. Or so he thought. "I don't need to be picked up."

"Oh, but I think you do."

He passed a slow-moving flatbed truck before resuming the debate. "You don't trust me?"

There was no point in denying the obvious. "Not any farther than I can throw you—and I'm pretty strong for my size," she added.

Picking up speed again, Kane spared his partner a glance. A few choice words rose to his lips, but he bit them back. However, the incredulous look on his face said it all.

"Right, you're a regular Hercules," he said with a dismissive laugh.

"That's not the image that immediately comes to mind," she told him. "But if it makes you happy I can live with it."

"What would make me happy is if you just cease and desist," he told her forcefully—not that that did any more good with her than it had with her predecessor, he was beginning to think.

"I guess you are right," she conceded. "We can't have everything we want."

Kane said something unintelligible under his breath. She thought it best to leave it that way. As her mother used to say, there was no sense in borrowing trouble.

Forty-five minutes later, Kane dropped her off in the parking lot beside her car.

"I'll see you tomorrow," Kelly told him as she got out of his vehicle.

"Threatening an officer of the law is a punishable offense," he quipped.

She grinned at him. "I'll still see you tomorrow. Good luck with whatever you're doing tonight," she added as an innocent afterthought.

It was neither innocent nor an afterthought.

Kane's expression instantly sobered.

She wondered if, just for a moment, whatever it

was that was bothering him had been moved to the background and, just temporarily, forgotten.

She would have asked him, but she already knew that wasn't going to get her anywhere. The man just refused to communicate with her.

Kelly fervently wished that the man driving away believed that sharing a problem helped to lighten the burden. Just for a second, it had struck her that he had the weight of the world on his shoulders. Broad or not, eventually that could break him. He needed to tell her what was bothering him.

But one small victory at a time was about all she could hope for.

With that she got into her car.

Chapter 12

He woke up disoriented to the sound of a ringing phone.

His phone.

Kane groped around on his nightstand for his phone while trying to keep his eyes closed for a couple of seconds longer.

The sun, shining into his bedroom, pried them open, just as his cell phone pried open his brain.

His first thought was that they had caught another case.

He put his phone to his ear.

"Durant," Kane announced, trying to remember what day of the week it was. His brain function was lagging behind.

The second he heard her voice the rest of his system came online. His brain was no longer fuzzy. It just felt as if it was under siege.

"Are you ready?"

Kane scrubbed his hand over his face. Bits and pieces of his life were pulling themselves together into a recognizable whole. "For you?" He laughed harshly. "Never."

Rather than take offense, Kelly said breezily, "Your chariot awaits, Cinderella."

Okay, maybe he was still asleep and having a nightmare, Kane thought. "What the hell are you talking about?"

"I'm here to take you to brunch—just like we talked about," Kelly cheerfully, albeit patiently, reminded her partner.

That wasn't the way he recalled it. "*You* talked. I said no."

"No. You didn't," she contradicted maddeningly. "You wisely surrendered because you knew I was right about this. You also knew I wasn't going to give up, so you held out for the best bargain, which is my doing your reports for a month. Ringing a bell yet?" she prodded.

Kane stuck to his guns. "Nope. None of this sounds even vaguely familiar," he replied.

Her tone shifted, telling him she wasn't going to continue playing games. "It doesn't have to sound familiar, you just have to comply. Now open your damn door."

Propping his phone up with his shoulder and the side of his head, he had his hands free. He grabbed his jeans and slid them on. He felt better prepared to handle things—and her—with clothes on.

"Why?" he asked.

"Because I'm standing right outside it waiting to take you to Andrew's for brunch," she told him patiently.

"And if I refuse to go?" he challenged.

"Don't make me use force," she threatened.

Wearing only his jeans and a bemused expression, Kane pulled opened the front door. Kelly was standing less than an inch away. Had she been leaning against the door, she would have fallen in at his feet.

For just half a second, he indulged himself with that fantasy: having her fall at his feet, necessitating his having to put his arms around her to pick her up...

The next moment, he shook himself free of the seductive thought and came back to reality and his apartment.

"Damn, you weren't kidding," he marveled. The woman really didn't give up easily.

"Nope, I wasn't. I'd give you fair warning if I was just pulling your leg." Her eyes swept over him. It was impossible to remain neutral to a man whose physique was the closest to perfect she had ever seen. "You might want to put something on before we go."

His amusement was definitely growing. "And if I don't?"

She shrugged. His bare chest was *not* a deal breaker. She knew of several cousins who would have judged it a real plus as far as livening up the gathering. "As long as you're comfortable, I guess it'll be okay. But one way or another you're coming with me, Durant, so stop fighting it."

Kane sighed. He had a feeling his partner was not above dumping his body into a wheelbarrow and running with him all the way to her uncle's house if it came down to that.

For a second he considered resisting just to see if he was right. But when he came right down to it, he had to admit that part of him—a very small part— was curious about these so-called famous gatherings that the former chief of police held.

"Give me a minute," he said in a less-than-cheerful voice. There was no point in letting her think she had won him over easily.

"I'm feeling generous. I'll give you two," she told him magnanimously.

Kane shot her a dark look and warned, "Don't push it."

She offered him a Cheshire-cat grin and said, "I wouldn't dream of it."

As if he believed her, Kane thought with a touch of cynicism.

* * *

Less than ten minutes later Kane was ready to go. Since it was Saturday, he was dressed even more casual than usual.

"Let's get this over with," he told her.

On some level he was looking forward to this, Kelly thought. If he wasn't, if he really didn't want to go, no power on earth—certainly not her—could get him to attend.

However, since he was obviously giving more than an inch, she could afford to do the same and play along. "Cheer up. You're going to enjoy this," she promised.

The look Kane gave her all but shouted, "We'll see about that."

"Still don't understand why my coming to brunch seems to be so important to you."

"I realize that," she acknowledged as she waited for him to lock up. "But you will. Eventually," she added, not wanting him to think that she expected some sort of an epiphany to transform him. It was that, just for a second the other day, she had glimpsed the little boy who had witnessed his entire family as well as his own innocence and trust being wiped out. She wanted, in some small way, to give a little of that back to him. Wanted him to be part of an actual family atmosphere for the space of a few hours.

She was firmly convinced that there was a healing

power in the kind of closeness her family enjoyed—
and it wasn't exclusive to family members.

For the most part Kane was quiet as she drove to
Andrew's development. For once she didn't try to
fill the silence with an outpouring of words. She let
him have his solitude.

It didn't take long to get there. Kelly parked her
vehicle as close to Andrew's house as she could.
Kane got out first and waited for her to join him.
Once she had, they began walking up the block.

"I've only got to do this once, right?" he questioned.

Kelly didn't hesitate, even though mentally she
crossed her fingers. "Right."

He studied her as he asked, "And then you'll leave
me alone."

"Absolutely," she promised, perhaps a tad too
quickly.

"Why don't I believe you?" he questioned.

In his opinion her shrug was just a little too innocent.

"Because you're not a very trusting man," she
speculated as they arrived at Andrew's front door.

The sound of raised, cheerful voices could be
heard through the heavy wooden door. It was a noisy
crowd, he caught himself thinking.

"That must be it," he quipped sarcastically.

At that moment the wide front door swung open. The noise and sounds of laughter increased twofold.

"So, you're Kelly's new partner," Andrew Cavanaugh said, taking Kane's hand and shaking it. "Been looking forward to meeting you," the former chief of police told him.

Kane hadn't expected to meet the man face-to-face so soon, nor was he sure exactly what he was supposed to say. So he just shook the older man's hand and murmured, "Nice to meet you, sir."

"How's your uncle doing?" Andrew asked, ushering them in. "Has retirement made him stir-crazy yet?" Andrew chuckled softly under his breath.

His interest seemed genuine, Kane found himself thinking.

"No, not yet," Kane answered, surprised that the former chief of police even knew who his uncle was. But the next words out of the clan patriarch's mouth convinced him that he did. "Tell Keith that if he ever decides he's had enough of the *ideal life* I've got a proposition for him."

"A proposition?" Kane repeated. "What sort of a proposition?"

"My dad and I run a security firm," Andrew told him. His father was still full of surprises, Andrew thought. Several years ago Seamus Cavanaugh had "unretired" himself and decided to start a small security business on the side. So far, knock on wood, it had been growing and progressing at a very healthy rate.

"Nothing fancy," Andrew continued. "But it keeps the day interesting for a few retired cops. Thought maybe Keith might enjoy rubbing elbows with some of the guys he knew back in the day. Tell him to come by if he's interested," Andrew urged.

"I will," Kane promised. That could be just the thing to get his uncle out of his malaise. Keith didn't do well without a purpose. And ever since retiring from the force, his uncle had had no structure, no direction. Only more time on his hands than he knew what to do with.

Kelly stood by silently listening to the exchange and noting the way her partner seemed suddenly to perk up. It was obvious that the way to the man's good side was by doing something for his uncle.

She could relate to that, Kelly thought. However, in her case it was her father she was always concerned about. When retirement came for him, she felt confident that Murdoch Cavanaugh was going to need to do something useful with himself. That was just the way the man was built.

Maybe he could look into joining this security firm, as well.

When Andrew had moved on to another one of his guests, she prodded, "So, this is turning out not to be so bad, right?"

Kane shrugged. "The jury's still out on that," he answered.

"On the contrary," she pointed out with more than

a little confidence. "The jury's already voted on that and everyone's happy with the outcome."

"So, she did it," a male voice belonging to someone standing behind Kane declared in surprise. "I didn't think she could nag you into coming."

Kane turned around to look at the man who was talking to him. The face, with its rugged features, high cheekbones and vivid green eyes, was vaguely familiar, and then, at the same time, it wasn't. But obviously the man knew Kelly.

"As the old saying goes, my partner can talk the ears off a brass monkey," Kane said in reply.

The man laughed heartily. "You're preaching to the choir, Detective. She damn near made mine fall off in self-defense."

"And you are?" Kane asked.

The young man extended his hand. "One of her long-suffering brothers. Bryce," he added, as if realizing that introductions—since this was a newcomer—were necessary. "At your service."

"Don't pay any attention to him," Kelly told her partner. "Bryce's actually one of the few men who are even grumpier than you are—at least at times."

Kane's eyes shifted toward the man he had just met. "Is she always this bluntly direct?"

Bryce laughed, obviously getting a kick out of the assessment.

"She's a straight shooter, our Kelly," Bryce assured him. "Sometimes a bit *too* straight a shooter.

She hasn't learned how to sugarcoat things yet. Maybe you can teach her a thing or two," Bryce suggested.

Kane allowed himself a moment to study the woman under discussion. "I don't think that anyone can teach your sister anything."

The remark *really* seemed to tickle Bryce. He grinned as he looked at his sister. "I guess your partner really does know you, doesn't he, Kel?"

Kelly turned up her nose at her brother, pretending to ignore him.

"Maybe you'd like to meet someone else," she suggested to Kane.

She hooked her arm through his and physically pulled him over to another cluster of people. People, she hoped, who wouldn't hand Kane any more material to use against her than he already had. Although, she knew what Bryce had said was all part of a calculated maneuver. Because she was still trying to figure Kane out, she couldn't be certain that any of her siblings would accidentally say or do something that would put her partner off and thus cause him to withdraw again.

All she could do at this point was hope for the best.

Kane would have preferred to stand and just observe, but he found that was not nearly as easy as it might have sounded. Apparently Cavanaughs didn't know the meaning of the word solitude or solitary. From what he could see, they were all about crowds of people mingling. If they saw a loner, he—or she—stirred a sudden need within a Cavanaugh to incorporate that loner into the whole.

"Resistance is futile," a phrase once popular in a science fiction show cult favorite, was very obviously a credo for getting on with the Cavanaughs as well, Kane couldn't help thinking.

"I can't find two solitary minutes to rub together," Kane complained when his path crossed Kelly's again a little while later. "Everyone keeps jumping in, talking to me, wanting to ask something, share something, or just plain talk at length on topics I never brought up. Are they always like this?"

"Like what?" she asked innocently.

Could she actually not know what he was referring to? Kane had his doubts, although if this was the way things had always been in her family, he could see how someone might be oblivious to it.

"Like someone wound them up and just let them run loose."

Her smile wasn't apologetic or sheepish. What it was, in the absolute sense, was proud. He could understand that. Every family member just wanted to be proud of their association with the other members of the clan. For the most part, he'd spent his youngest years deprived of that. And while his uncle was far from the warmest man ever created, Kane *had* become a law enforcement agent to cull his favor and gain his approval.

"Pretty much," Kelly had to acknowledge. "They watch out for one another." Because what she'd just said sounded wrong to her ear, or rather it sounded incomplete, Kelly corrected herself and said, "*We* watch out for one another." She peered at his face a bit more closely, doing her best not to be distracted by features that would have made a nun entertain thoughts of leaving her order. Instead, she focused on what she saw beneath all that. "You want to leave, don't you?"

He had, but that had been when they'd first arrived and he'd felt like an outsider. The people around him—his partner's people—had quickly erased that feeling for him. "Oddly enough, no. At least not yet." He stopped talking, searching for the right words, and then decided there really weren't any, at least none that would correctly express what he was feeling. "This isn't what I expected," he confessed.

"And what is it that you expected?" Kelly asked, all the while taking small bites of what she felt was an amazing piece of French toast.

"To be nauseated in under sixty seconds. Five minutes, tops." He shook his head when she offered him a piece of the French toast. She chose to override him and managed to get a forkful between his lips. She had to admit that caused a small, warm, delicious little shiver to go racing up her spine. From the one unguarded look she'd seen on his face, sampling the small piece she'd gotten into his mouth had been an entirely pleasurable event for Kane.

She struggled to hide her smile. "Are you disappointed that you're not nauseous?"

He was definitely *not* disappointed. It seemed that nothing that had to do with the Cavanaughs was simple or cut-and-dried.

"Stunned is more like it."

She nodded. "*Stunned*'s a good word. I'll take that," she told him. He didn't look stunned, she thought. If she was to judge by his appearance, he seemed pleased. They were getting to him, getting through that armor he kept around himself.

Just as she had hoped.

And then she decided to pry just a little. "I heard Andrew asking about your uncle. Did he retire recently?"

"Not recently," he told her "It's been a few years." And he was clearly surprised that the family patriarch, with an ever-expanding family of Cavanaughs to keep track of, still knew that he was related to Keith and had actually kept up on the man's life. Surprised and maybe just a little bit glad, as well.

Kane had caught himself looking at his partner in unguarded moments, having his imagination wander off with him. He found himself wondering if by some wild chance things would heat up between them, and, if they did, what repercussions that sort of thing might have on them, on him and on his career.

He had no idea why that thought had suddenly turned up in his head. Nor why he couldn't immediately terminate it instead of exploring it from all sides.

As if reactions could all be neatly labeled, cataloged and annotated for future generations.

They couldn't, and he of all people knew that.

Still, Kane decided that perhaps hanging around a little while longer in this hub of socializing Cavanaughs wouldn't be all that bad an idea. He could think of it as doing reconnaissance.

It never hurt to know his enemy—and if it turned out that Kelly Cavanaugh *wasn't* his enemy, look at all the intel gathering that had been accomplished. If nothing else, it was good practice. Not to mention that it allowed him to gain insight into a branch of the Cavanaughs that his partner interacted with closely. Getting to know them would be invaluable in giving him a clue as to what exactly made this partner of his tick.

All in all, Kane stayed a great deal longer than he had initially intended. And he learned things. Learned that despite his tendency to keep to himself, he actually liked these people, who didn't allow natural boundaries to force them to remain on the outside, looking in. They very boldly abandoned the outside for the inside, politely but firmly infiltrating the world of anyone who had the unique fortune of being around them.

His natural instinct was to close up, but he found that, astonishingly enough, he didn't want to. Not in this case. These people were fellow cops who very obviously—or, in a few cases, not so obviously—cared about the people they brought into their lives. Ordinarily, he didn't like anyone prying into his life. Cavanaughs pried all the time. And the damn thing about it was that it didn't faze him.

That alone should have had him heading for the hills. But it didn't. He told himself he had time for that later, that he could always shut down and walk away at a moment's notice.

A moment of his own choosing.

But for now it suited him to stick around and observe them.

Observe her.

Because his partner was getting to him more and more—something that should have put him on his guard—he told himself that he could put emotional distance between the two of them anytime he wanted to.

He just didn't *want* to at this present time.

Not until he was ready.

Chapter 13

"Uncle Andrew wants to know when you're coming back."

It was a couple of weeks after he had shared brunch with his partner, the former chief of police and a good number of Cavanaughs, and they were traveling to the scene of yet another home invasion in the upscale section of Aurora. The count was now up to seven—including this latest one—and they were still no closer to closing in on a viable suspect than they had been a month earlier.

Kane was driving and, in her opinion, he took his sweet time answering her question. He took so long she thought he was going to ignore it, so she was about to pointedly ask him again when he finally spoke.

"In case you haven't noticed, I'm kind of busy here with these home invasions."

"*We're* kind of busy," Kelly corrected. "And yes, I noticed. I also noticed something else." She paused, waiting for Kane to jump in with the logical question following her statement. When he didn't, she took it upon herself to pretend that she was Kane and answered for him. "'What else did you notice, Kelly?' Glad you asked, Kane. What I noticed is that we still have to eat, which is where the matter of stopping by the chief's place comes in. The meal'll be already made. We stop, eat and run. Oddly enough, the chief has no problem with that. The only thing he has a problem with is if someone deliberately doesn't show up even though the invitation is out there on the table for him."

Kelly paused again, waiting for her partner to make some sort of a comment. When he still didn't, she prodded, "Well? *Say* something."

He spared her a pointed look. "I don't call you by your first name."

She stared at him. "What?"

"In that little miniplay you just performed, when you were putting words into my mouth, you had me referring to you by your first name. I don't do that," he told her, his voice devoid of emotion.

He'd hooked on to something minor and inconsequential, all in an effort not to talk about the real issue. "Maybe that's the problem."

Kane sighed, frustrated. "I wasn't aware that there was a problem—other than our not being able to hone in on a suspect committing these home invasions," he added.

"The problem," she emphasized, "is that you're desperately trying to keep those damn walls up, keeping everyone out. My family put a decent-size crack in those walls and that worries you, I know it does." Which was why he was staying away, she thought.

"And why is that?" Kane asked sarcastically.

He wanted her to spell it out for him. Well, she was happy to oblige. "You're worried that if you let those walls come down, if you allow yourself to get close to someone and let them get close to you, you'll be setting yourself up to be really disappointed and hurt somewhere down the line." She paused for a second before adding, "Like you were as a kid."

Kane shot her a look she couldn't quite read. "Ready to hang up your shingle, Dr. Freud?"

It was all or nothing. He needed to know that she knew. They had to get that out of the way before she could get him to open up and allow her in. It would be easier just to back away, but being there for someone wasn't about easy, it was about commitment.

"I know, Kane," she said quietly.

"Know?" he repeated as if she'd used a foreign

word he'd never heard before. "What is it that you know, Cavanaugh?"

Kelly took a breath and then let out everything she'd been holding back. Mentally, she crossed her fingers that she wasn't making a really bad mistake.

"I know that your father killed your mother and thought he'd killed you just before he killed himself. You survived something that no one, especially a kid, should have to go through, but you did survive," she emphasized. "There had to be a reason."

"Yeah," he said, his voice dripping with sarcasm. "The old man didn't hit anything vital and I lived."

"You *lived* for a reason," Kelly insisted. "You went on to make something of your life, to make a difference. But that scared boy inside, that little boy who saw his immediate world go up in flames, he's still in there trying single-handedly to hold down the fort while keeping the entire world at bay."

"You finished?" Kane demanded in a monotone voice.

"Almost. I'm here for you, Kane," she stressed. "Anytime you want to talk, to unload, to rant, I'm here. And so's my family. We're all very good at listening, and we're not going to disappoint you," she added before saying, "*Now* I'm finished."

"Just in time," he commented.

When she looked at him quizzically, he pointed to the house that had a patrol car parked in front of it as well as a couple of officers taking down a woman's statement.

"We're here," he said.

Kelly frowned. He was doing it again. He was evading her. But there *was* a job to do and a new victim to question in hopes of gleaning some piece of information that would finally point them in the right direction. They definitely needed to discover just who was behind this rash of home invasions.

"We'll pick this up later," Kelly promised as they got out of the sedan.

Kane made no reply.

The latest victim, Ellis Johnson, was a highly successful investment broker who believed in living lavishly and spent his money accordingly. He was livid over what had happened to him and had no problem saying so when questioned about the details of the home invasion.

"If it wasn't for his damn gun, I would have overpowered him," he told Kane, contempt seething out of every pore.

"So the thief who broke into your house was on the small side?" Kelly asked.

Johnson, who appeared to be in the neighborhood of six-four, drew himself up to his full height and said, "Hell, yes. I could have picked him up and thrown him against the wall if I could have gotten my hands on him. But he was waving around that gun and he looked crazy enough to use it."

Kane was instantly alert. "Then you saw his face?" he questioned.

"No," Johnson grumbled. "But I saw his eyes. They had this really crazy look in them." Scowling, he cursed viciously. "Do you know what that bastard did?"

"Why don't you tell us?" Kelly said, doing her best to sound sympathetic. It wasn't easy. She was beginning to understand why someone would want to do something drastic to teach the broker a lesson in humility.

"That bastard took down my paintings right in front of me. My very expensive art treasures," he emphasized. "And he destroyed them! Stood right there, two feet away from me, and slashed the canvas with a knife! I could have ripped him apart with my bare hands." Talking about it now had caused his face to turn a bright shade of red.

"Was there *anything* that was even vaguely familiar about him?" Kelly pressed. "Anything that stood out?"

"He was a nobody," Johnson spat out. "Not somebody I would have noticed. He was like all the other nobodies in this world. Transparent even while they're standing in front of you. How can you expect me to remember a nobody like that?"

"Well, for one thing, this nobody destroyed your Turner seascape," Kane reminded the victim.

His face turned even redder. "For that alone he should get a lethal injection," the broker raged.

"Yeah, well, first we have to find him," Kane said, more to himself than to the victim.

Just then Kane's phone began to ring. He slid it out of his pocket to check the caller ID. A hint of confusion entered his expression. Glancing up at his partner, he said, "I have to take this."

Not waiting for Kelly to say anything one way or another, he turned away and took several steps to the side for privacy.

"This isn't interesting enough for you?" Johnson accused, raising his voice for Kane's benefit.

Kelly was quick to divert the victim's attention to herself. "Every case we get interests us, Mr. Johnson. What happened to you seems to be part of a rash of home invasions."

The man looked astonished and then angry. "This is an ongoing investigation? And you haven't figured it out yet? What am I paying taxes for?"

"For a great many things, Mr. Johnson," Kelly told him as patiently as she could. "And just for your own information, solving a case isn't done in forty-nine minutes—not counting commercials—the way it is on TV. We're piecing things together and comparing each home invasion to all the others in the state that have taken place."

Johnson snorted with contempt. "Seems to me that your department could do with some better detectives. Who do I call about that?" he asked, sounding belligerent.

Kelly congratulated herself on keeping her smile—as well as her temper—intact.

"Anyone you want to." Out of the corner of her eye, she saw Kane closing his cell phone and slipping it back into his pocket. He appeared agitated and disturbed. "Excuse me," she told the broker just before she walked away from him.

"No, I will not excuse you," Johnson shouted. "I want to know who the hell is going to pay for my trashed painting!"

"Your insurance company comes to mind," Kelly said, tossing the words over her shoulder. Catching up to Kane, she asked, "Is everything all right?"

For a second he seemed surprised to see her. Obviously distracted, he said, "Yeah, fine. Look, I have go."

"Go? Go where?" she asked, catching hold of his arm. She had a feeling that if she hadn't, he'd just keep walking without saying anything further.

Kane disengaged himself from her. "I have to go take care of something. You finish questioning Mr. Personality over there. Get his full statement. I've got to take the car, so catch a ride with one of the uniforms. Thanks," he added automatically.

"Where can I reach you?" she asked, calling after

him. But Kane had already left Johnson's house and was out of earshot.

She wanted to run after him, to offer her help with whatever it was that had him so upset, but she knew he would refuse her.

Squaring her shoulders and taking a deep, fortifying breath, Kelly turned around and headed back to the less than cooperative broker. He was glaring at her expectantly, as if he thought she should have the apprehended thief in hand.

"Why don't I have you write down exactly what you just told me?" Kelly suggested once she was next to Johnson.

This was obviously *not* what Johnson had in mind. He looked at her with absolute disdain. "You want me to include pictures, as well?"

It was a struggle, but she didn't allow her real feelings to come through. Instead, she offered Johnson her very best, brightest smile. "No, just the words will do."

With that she put some distance between herself and the home invasion victim. Her self-restraint was within minutes of being flung out the window.

If they went according to a list of people the broker had undoubtedly alienated, Kelly doubted if they would be finished questioning everyone within a year. The man had one of the most abrasive personalities she had ever encountered. She thought of herself as mild mannered and even *she* was tempted to destroy something of Johnson's just to put the obnoxious man in his place. That feeling had to be intensified among the people who actually knew and had to deal with him.

After taking down all the information she could and leaving the crime scene investigators to photograph the scene, Kelly hitched a ride with a patrol officer to the precinct.

The first thing she noticed as she crossed the lot was that Kane's car was missing. Wherever he had gone, he was still there, she concluded.

When she tried to call him on his cell, her call went straight to voice mail. Kane's phone must have been off.

Frustrated, Kelly forced herself to focus on this latest home invasion case. She meticulously placed key points on the board that was already set up with information from the other six home invasions.

She stayed at it for as long as she could, trying to find just one common thread that ran between all the victims. But again, this latest victim had little to nothing in common with the others. And whatever she did find that two of the victims had in common, it did not carry over to the rest of the group. They used different salons, different gardeners, different dry cleaners, etc. After a while, it felt like an exercise in futility.

The only thing that all the home invasion victims had in common was their ages. She kept coming back to that.

That had to mean something, didn't it? She just couldn't really hone in on what.

But in all honesty, her mind was not completely dedicated to the details of the robberies. Part of her was preoccupied with an entirely different matter. She kept waiting for Kane to either turn up in the squad room or at the very least return her call.

Neither happened.

She was acting like a schoolgirl, she chided herself. He was her partner, not some high school hunk she had a crush on. Yet she couldn't deny that she felt this funny tingle washing over her every time someone walked in and for a second or so, she thought it was him.

Grow up, Kelly!

Frustrated, Kelly left yet another voice mail on his smartphone. In addition, she tried texting Kane, as well.

Where the hell are you? I could use your input on our case right now. This is no time to take a break. You can walk on water later.

Even her pseudo rebuke didn't get any sort of a response from her missing partner.

Where *was* he?

Something was definitely wrong. Kelly could feel it in her bones.

On her way home she detoured and drove past her Kane's apartment complex.

His parking space was empty and no lights were on in his apartment. Even so, she went to his door and knocked. She got no answer. At this point, she hadn't expected one.

After making sure no one was watching her, Kelly deftly picked the lock—something she had learned from Brennan, who'd learned it during his under-cover days.

Afterward she turned the doorknob and let her-self in.

A quick tour of the premises told her what her gut already knew. Kane wasn't there.

Kelly closed up the apartment and went back to her vehicle, reviewing the options she had available to her. She could stay here in visitor parking and wait for Kane to come back and then flee again, or—

The *or* jumped up at her like an unexpected sun-rise. Before she thought better of it, she quickly put in a call to Valri.

The second she heard the other end of the line being picked up, Kelly blurted out, "I need another favor."

Valri laughed drily. "And a hello to you, too, Kelly."

"Hi," Kelly replied automatically. "The precinct's

vehicles have a way of tracking down their where-
abouts on them, right?"

"Right," Valri said cautiously. "Why are you asking about that? You didn't lose the car, did you?" she
asked, horrified.

"No, I didn't lose it. Kane took off in it. I need to
find out where Kane is now," she said bluntly.

"Why don't you just call him?"

"If I could call him, don't you think I would?"
Kelly asked impatiently. "He got a call in the middle of our investigation and just took off. I need to
know where he is."

"Kelly," Valri began, a warning note in her voice.

Kelly had no time for lectures on patience and
proper behavior. That was for downtime, not now.
"Val, please. I wouldn't ask if this wasn't important."

"Yeah, you would," Valri contradicted. "Does this
have anything to do with police business?"

Valri was asking because she had to, Kelly realized. "Yes. Yes, it does. I have to warn him about
something our latest victim just told me."

Kelly couldn't help wondering if that excuse she
had just made up sounded as lame to Valri as it did
to her.

"Okay, hang on. Let me see if I can locate his
vehicle."

It took Valri several minutes of flipping through
potential databases before she finally found what

she was looking for and was able to isolate the vehicle's coordinates.

"Got it!" Valri declared triumphantly. "According to what I have here, it says that your partner's vehicle is parked in a lot at Aurora General Hospital."

"A hospital?"

Had he been in an accident? But something like that would have made the news stations, she thought. Certainly any police-involved accident would have been broadcasted over the police scanners.

"Thanks, Valri," Kelly said, "You're an angel. I'll take it from here."

Valri started to say something, then stopped. The dial tone in her ear told her that she was talking to herself.

Kelly had terminated the call.

Chapter 14

It took Kelly several minutes to locate her partner's sedan.

She finally found it parked not too far from the hospital's admissions entrance. Since the vehicle was there rather than parked in the smaller lot strictly reserved for emergency patients, Kelly assumed that whoever Kane had come to see had been admitted to Aurora General.

Parking her car as close to his as possible, given that the lot was more than three-quarters full, Kelly mentally crossed her fingers that she was somehow going to be able to find what floor Kane was on and what room he'd gone to.

The only other alternative she had was to remain

in her car and wait for Kane to come out and get into his vehicle. The flaw in that plan was if Kane opted to stay the night keeping vigil, either in a waiting room or in someone's hospital room, she would be out of luck and no closer to knowing what was going on with her partner than she was right at this moment.

Kelly got out of her car.

After walking into the hospital, she looked around and spotted the long admissions desk. It was divided up into three partitions, each with its own clerk.

She picked the one closest to the hospital entrance, thinking that Kane might have done the same thing.

Approaching the first desk, she flashed a smile at the woman in the pink smock and dived in. "Did a rather tall, good-looking man come in here within the last hour or so looking for someone who was admitted to your hospital in, say, the last twelve hours?"

There, Kelly thought, *that should cover all the bases.*

The clerk, a motherly, jovial-faced woman who looked as if she spent her off-hours whipping up bakery goods, shook her head.

"Honey, even if I *could* tell you—and the privacy laws say I can't—I'm afraid you'd have to give me more to work with than just that."

Kelly took a breath, telling herself to focus. Being scattered like this just wasn't like her.

"Okay, let's start over," she suggested. Taking out

her wallet, Kelly showed the woman her badge as well as her ID. "I'm Detective Kelly Cavanaugh. The man I'm looking for is Detective Kane Durant. He would have identified himself." Suddenly, she remembered Andrew asking after Kane's uncle Keith. If something had happened to Kane's uncle, that would have sent him rushing to the hospital, she thought. "He'd be asking about someone who had been recently admitted as an inpatient. An older man named Keith."

"Keith what?" the woman asked her, typing a few commands to pull up the new patients database.

Kelly didn't have a clue as to the man's last name. Valri hadn't passed on that information.

"I don't know," she admitted. "Could you just go through the most recent admissions in the last twelve hours?" It was possible that the man might have been admitted earlier and the hospital had just now notified Kane, but for the time being, she didn't want to think about that.

The woman behind the desk looked skeptical. Clearing her throat, she told her, "This is highly irregular."

"The man you admitted is my partner's only living relative. I just wanted to be there to lend him some support," she told the older woman, whose nameplate identified her as Marjorie White. "Could you just take one quick look? Please, Marjorie?"

The woman glanced to either side of the cubicle

where she was seated, not that anyone actually could crane their necks far enough to be able to see what she was pulling up on her screen.

"Give me a minute," she whispered, her fingers flying along the keyboard.

It took less than a minute.

In exactly twenty-eight seconds, Marjorie had pulled up the necessary information. "A Keith Leeds was admitted an hour ago from the ER." The woman raised her eyes from the monitor to look at Kelly. "He was in a car accident, and it says here that he's presently in a coma."

"Omigod," Kelly whispered, stunned as well as concerned. Kane had to be devastated. Why hadn't he said anything before taking off? "Can I have his room number, please?"

"He's in room 241. It's right across from ICU. They were out of beds," Marjorie explained. "We admitted the survivors of a multicar pileup on I-5 yesterday afternoon."

As sorry as she was to hear about that accident, the one that concerned her was the one that had involved Kane's uncle and had brought him here.

"Thank you," Kelly said as she started for the elevators.

"Send me a wedding picture," the woman called after her.

Marjorie's parting words had Kelly stopping dead in her tracks. She quickly retraced her steps to the admission's clerk. What was the woman talking about?

"Detective Durant is my partner at work," she specified. "We're not a couple."

But the smile on the matronly woman's face told Kelly that she obviously thought otherwise.

"You keep telling yourself that, honey. But that look in your eyes says something else. I've had a lot of couples pass through here over the years. Some of them on the worst day of their lives. I know all the signs of involvement."

"I'm just concerned how this'll affect his job performance, that's all," she assured the woman.

"Uh-huh."

Kelly started to protest further, but then decided that it just wasn't worth it. She didn't have time to try to convince a woman she was, in all likelihood, never going to see again. Her only concern right now was Kane. Macho loner or not, he had to be beside himself about this. And he had no one to turn to.

Or so he thought. She wanted to let him know that she was there for him.

When the elevator did not appear the moment she pressed for it, Kelly decided to take the stairs.

She raced up the metal steps, the heels of her shoes clicking almost rhythmically against them. When she emerged from the stairwell and into the hallway, it took her a second to get her bearings.

After passing the nurse's station, she followed the arrows on the wall.

The door to room 241 was partially open and she peered in before entering. Just as she surmised, Kane was there, sitting in a padded bright orange chair and looking at the man in the hospital bed. She saw that the man's eyes were closed, and a variety of tubes were in his arm, some hooked up to a cluster of machines that in turn were monitoring a host of bodily functions.

"How is he?" Kelly asked as she entered the room.

She'd startled him. She could see that by the momentarily unguarded look on Kane's face. He recovered quickly.

"What the hell are you doing here?" he asked. There was a note of irritation in the whispered question.

"Asking you how your uncle is," she replied innocently. Why couldn't he just accept her concern? Why did everything have to turn into a verbal duel? "I'm a better detective than you give me credit for," she told him simply.

"And now you can just *detective* yourself home," Kane told her. It was obvious that he thought she was going to comply.

Partnered for a few weeks and the man still didn't know her, Kelly thought.

"If you don't mind, I think I'll stay for a while,"

she told him. She kept her voice mild, but it was obvious she had no intention of going anywhere.

There was another chair in the room, shoved over in the corner and out of the way. Kelly claimed it and sank down on the seat.

"Why would you want to do that?" Kane asked impatiently. "Why would you want to stay here, watching him breathe? It doesn't make any sense. You don't even know him."

"No," Kelly readily agreed, "but I know you, and I think that you could use some emotional support right about now."

"I'm fine," Kane told her, all but growling the words.

"And you'll be *finer* with company," she replied, smiling at him sweetly.

Kane looked as if he wanted to say a few choice words, but then bit them back. "You are damn stubborn, you know that?" It was an accusation.

"I know," she answered cheerfully. "It's part of my charm."

"Not hardly," he retorted under his breath, but loud enough for her to hear.

Because of the nature of the situation, she was prepared to cut Kane a lot of slack. If that were her only living relative, she didn't know how civil she would be, given that she would be almost crazy with worry.

Kelly gazed at the unconscious man in the hospital bed. "Have you spoken to the doctor yet?"

Kane didn't bother to look at her. All his attention was focused on his uncle, on watching him breathe and fervently hoping he would continue to do so.

"Yes."

When he didn't say anything further, she prodded, "And?"

Kane shrugged, a great deal of helplessness evident in the single small gesture.

"And he could come out of it at any minute—or he could stay like this for the rest of his life." The words weighed heavily on his tongue. "They're not really sure."

She tried to think of all the logical questions that needed to be answered. "Did they operate on him?" was the first one.

Kane scrubbed his hand over his face, as if that could somehow help him pull himself together.

"Yeah. They said they think they stopped all the internal bleeding." She saw frustration in his eyes as he looked up at her. "They *think*," he repeated, jeering at the word, making it sound like it was a definite liability.

Kelly did what she could to reassure her partner. "This is a really good hospital," she told him. "Plenty of police officers have gotten patched up here and returned to duty, good as new. I can personally vouch for a bunch of them," she said, thinking of all the times one of her relatives had landed on the operating table.

"Younger police officers," Kane emphasized. "Keith's going to be seventy…"

It was clear that the man's age worried him. Kelly did what she could to reassure him. "And you'll be with him to help him blow out the candles on his next birthday cake."

"You can't know that," he told her flatly.

"Know that for a fact? No. But I can believe it with all my heart." She needed to make him understand how important it was to hang on to positive thoughts. "Positive energy really does have its benefits, Kane. Doctors have made an actual study of the positive effects of positive thinking," she told him.

He shook his head, partially irritated and partially grateful for her bullheadedness. "You don't give up, do you?"

"What's the fun in that?" she asked.

The next minute, Kelly rose to her feet.

"Leaving?" he asked. He'd been trying to make her go, but now that she looked as if she was going to comply, he found himself feeling let down.

What the hell was going on with him? He didn't need anyone's support, he reminded himself. He'd gotten along fine without it so far.

"No, I'm not leaving," she answered. "I'm just going to get some coffee for us and see what they have in the vending machine. I skipped dinner. Can I get you anything?"

He ran his hand along the back of his neck, wishing he could somehow get rid of the tight knots he felt there. "Yeah, some of that positive energy you were talking about."

The smile she flashed him was almost beatific. "That'll take finding an extra special vending machine, but I'll see what I can do," Kelly promised.

"Go home, Cavanaugh."

When she looked up, she found that Kane was standing over her. He obviously had to have been shaking her arm to get her to wake up.

When had she fallen asleep? She didn't remember doing that. But she must have.

Stifling a yawn, she told him, "Can't get rid of me that easily."

"We can't both be out from work," he told her. "Not while we still have that home invasion case to solve." He pulled her chair slightly over to the side to get her to stand up. "Be sensible for once in your life. Go home and get some sleep. I can't have you falling asleep while you're driving because of me," he told her. There was no room left for argument.

Rotating her shoulders—God, but they ached— she glanced at her watch. The display told her that it was three in the morning.

Kane's uncle was still unconscious. There had been no change.

She rose from the chair and stretched. Kane was right. He was the relative, she had no reason to call in and someone did have to work the case.

She briefly laid her hand on Kane's shoulder. "Okay, call me when he comes to," she requested. "If there's no change, I'll be back tonight."

The fact that she had said "when" not "if" was not lost on Kane. The woman really *was* a Polly-anna, wasn't she?

"You don't have to," Kane told her.

Kelly put her hands to her ears and announced, "Sorry, can't hear you." With that, she made her way to the door.

Raising his voice, Kane called after her, "Hey, Cavanaugh—"

With one hand on the doorknob, Kelly looked at him over her shoulder and waited.

"Thanks."

All but melting, she smiled at him.

"No problem," she answered, knowing that any-thing more personal than that would only cause Kane discomfort.

Kelly headed into her day operating on adrena-line, coffee and very little else. But for now it was more than enough. As a matter of fact, she felt as if she had gotten her second wind.

Mercifully, there were no new reports of home invasions. The number remained at seven. She spent her time organizing the information on the board, hoping that something would suddenly jump out and hit her.

But it didn't.

The only thing that still remained vaguely constant in all the cases was the age range of the victims. Maybe the key to all this *was* in their background.

At any rate, with nothing new to concentrate on, it was worth pursuing a little.

Running a background check on all the invasion victims not only would be tedious, it also would undoubtedly take a long time. There were loads of cases ahead of hers waiting for the senior tech wizard Brenda Cavanaugh's magic touch. The chief of ds' daughter-in-law was swamped. And she couldn't lean on Valri again. Her sister was very good at getting computers to give up their secrets, but she had her own job at the police department and she couldn't be expected to drop everything to do her a favor. It wasn't fair to Valri.

But she also needed more information on all her victims. She decided to go to the horse's mouth in this case.

Kelly worked up a questionnaire for all the victims to fill out, asking for various pieces of information, such as where they had been born, where they had received their elementary and high school educations, what colleges they attended, etc.

She ran off more than enough copies of the questionnaire, then, armed with the papers, she went to reconnect with the victims.

"Is this thing even legal?" Johnson asked, rereading the one page questionnaire for the third time. He frowned more deeply with each pass he made.

"Just think of it as a simple survey," Kelly urged, then explained. "We're just trying to narrow down the playing field so that we can pinpoint just where and when your path and the thief's path crossed."

Johnson looked disgusted. "This is a big waste of time."

"Very little time," Kelly contradicted, holding up the single page as if she were conducting a reality check on the man.

His scowl deepened, all but disappearing into the folds around his neck. "You expect me to do it right now?"

Once again she hunted up her very brightest smile. "Please?" she said, secretly hating every second of her impromptu performance. "Everyone else has already filled out their questionnaire," she lied. "We just need yours to complete the set."

After liberally bestowing several colorful curses on her, the investment broker finally and grudgingly filled out the form.

* * *

She told each of the victims the same story, saying that theirs was the last form and that it was needed in order to make a comparison.

Eventually—after having to return twice to talk to Edward Mitchum—she had forms from all the victims.

Kelly scanned all the forms into her smartphone so she had a full second copy—just in case. Then since it was well past her shift, rather than process the results at the precinct, she took the originals with her to the hospital.

If Kane's uncle hadn't regained consciousness yet—and she assumed he hadn't since she had received no phone calls to that effect—she was fairly certain Kane could use some company. Even if he refused to admit it.

A sense of excitement pervaded her. She wasn't sure if it was because she was onto something with her questionnaire or if it was because she was heading to the hospital to keep Kane company.

Most likely, she told herself, it was a combination of both.

Chapter 15

Peering into the hospital room, Kelly saw that her partner's head was down, and it looked as if he had dozed off while keeping vigil at his uncle's bedside. Watching Kane carefully for any signs of movement, she took great pains not to make any noise as she tiptoed into the private unit.

All but moving in slow motion, Kelly took the large shoulder bag she'd crammed with the completed questionnaires as well as her laptop and deposited it onto the other chair in the room.

"You know, you can make noise. I'm not asleep," Kane said without looking up in her direction.

She'd been so intent on not making a sound that, when her partner spoke, she practically jumped. Her hand covered her chest as if to keep her heart from leaping out.

After taking a breath to compose herself, Kelly told him, "Well, I thought you were and I didn't want to disturb you."

Kane laughed drily. "You're a few weeks too late in that department." Sitting up straighter, he scrutinized her for a long moment. "The chief of ds and his wife stopped by here around noon to check on Keith's condition. You know anything about that?"

As far as he was concerned, it was a rhetorical question, but he wanted to see what Kelly would say when confronted with it.

Kelly's shrug was vague and noncommittal. "I *might* have mentioned to him in passing that your uncle was in the hospital."

"In passing," Kane echoed, not buying her story. "And just when did you do this *passing*?"

Kelly gave up the ruse. "Or, I could have just called him up with the information. The chief is close to his officers and detectives. And it doesn't matter to him if they're active or if they put in their papers years ago," she added before Kane could bring up the fact that his uncle was retired.

"It seems the chief subscribes to the same theory as you do," Kane told her. When she looked at him blankly, he elaborated. "The chief gave me a message to give to Keith when he wakes up—not if, but when. Looks to me like all of you Cavanaughs believe in miracles."

"You make it sound like it's a bad thing," she accused, then pointed out, "There's nothing wrong with expecting the best."

He had a different take on that. "There is if the worst happens."

She shook her head. She just didn't operate that way. "There's plenty of time to feel awful if that comes to pass. Besides," she maintained, "I told you what positive energy can do."

His eyes met hers. "Yes, drive a logical person crazy," he declared. But then he reconsidered his statement and his harsh stand in view of what she'd done for his uncle by telling the chief of ds about Keith's accident. In a somewhat humbler voice, Kane said, "Again, thanks."

Her eyes seemed to light up right in front of him as she said, "My pleasure."

Kane shook his head, more in wonder than in denial. The woman was one of a kind. He *really* wished she wasn't so attractive.

"You know, I actually believe that," he told her. And then, because he was getting too close both to her and to the feelings he always tried to keep in check, he asked, "How's the case coming? Any new home invasions?"

At least she could give him a little positive news, so to speak. "None, thank God."

"Anything new at all?"

Moving her shoulder bag to the floor, Kelly sat down in the other chair. "No, but I think there's something old we're overlooking. The only thing these people have in common is they're all around the same age." Something that they'd already mentioned. "I've been thinking maybe they all attended the same school somewhere along the line. I had them all fill out a general questionnaire."

The same school might have been a connection, but it didn't point to any reason why they were all victims, Kane thought.

"So what did you find?" he asked.

"I haven't had a chance to look the questionnaires over yet. But I did bring them with me. I thought you might want to take a crack at them, as well. See if anything occurs to you."

After opening the shoulder bag, Kelly removed the nine pages she had collected from the victims. She rose from her chair and brought the pages over to Kane.

"You brought me a pretty girl," a low, raspy voice said. Neither one of them had seen Keith open his eyes. It sounded as if he wanted to chuckle but couldn't. "Just what I wanted."

The words were spoken so softly that had the machines not been in a temporary lull as they rested before starting on their next complete cycle, neither Kane nor his partner would have heard anything.

Afraid that he'd imagined it, Kane was immediately on his feet and at the man's side. Frantically, he searched the deathly still face for any signs, however minute, of consciousness.

Taking the man's wide hand in his, Kane whispered, "Uncle Keith?"

To his overwhelming relief, Kane saw the man's chest move up and then down in a halting but definitely rhythmic pattern.

"You haven't called me Uncle Keith since you were a little boy," Keith said, a paper-thin smile attempting to curve at least a portion of his lips. He opened his eyes again, and it was obvious he was trying very hard to get his bearings. Shifting slightly in the bed, he groaned from the pain. "Where am I and why do I feel like I got hit by a train?"

"You're in the hospital," Kane told him. "And you feel like that because you were in a car accident. Witnesses said the other guy came out of nowhere and slammed into you before taking off."

It was a clear case of hit-and-run and whoever was responsible better hope that someone else found him and brought him in, Kane thought. Because if he did, he wasn't sure he could refrain from mopping the floor with the coward. Only a coward would do something like that and then flee rather than own up to it.

"Beatrice?" Keith asked in a hushed whisper.

She was about to ask Kane who that was when

he answered his uncle's question as well as her own by saying, "She's totaled."

Beatrice was the car, Kelly realized. She couldn't picture the tall, thin man in the hospital bed naming his ride.

"Damn," Keith bit off. "I always liked her."

"At least you'll live to get a new one," Kane told the man. "The chief of detectives was here, along with his wife."

Keith nodded, or made a movement that passed for nodding. "Lila," he acknowledged. "Damn fine cop in her day."

"They said to tell you that the precinct is taking up a collection to help pay for your physical therapy sessions."

Keith tried to nod again. This time he wound up wincing. "Guess then I'd better get well."

"Looks that way," Kane agreed.

Kelly noted the slight hitch in her partner's voice as he regarded his uncle, but she pretended she hadn't. However, she couldn't keep the smile from her face.

That was when Keith looked at her again. "And who is this lovely lady?" he asked his nephew.

Kane remembered hearing that in his day his uncle had been considered quite a ladies' man. "This is my partner. Kelly Cavanaugh."

Keith's eyes narrowed just a little, as if he was studying her. "Any relation to Brian Cavanaugh?"

"Every relation," she replied with a wide smile. "He's one of my granduncles." She placed her hand ever so lightly on top of his. "It is *very* nice to meet you, Mr. Leeds."

"Given the alternative, yes," Keith agreed, his voice fading a tad more. And then the man fell asleep before he could say another word.

"Looks like your uncle's going to make it," Kelly said.

About to go into the hallway to find a nurse to alert regarding his uncle's change in status, he stopped and turned to face Kelly. "Go ahead, say it."

"Say what?" she asked, not quite following him.

"'I told you so.'"

"I wouldn't dream of it," she answered with a smile that was big enough to encompass both of them—with room to spare.

As she watched, she saw that Kane had become awash in emotion, unable to say anything at all for a moment.

At a loss as how to help him deal with what he was feeling right now, all Kelly could do was place a comforting hand on his shoulder.

Something seemed to break inside of him when he felt her hand resting lightly there. All the things he'd been holding back, trying to deal with or, more accurately, to submerge, just came pouring out, all but drowning him.

Before he knew what was going on, he'd taken

hold of Kelly's arm, spun her right into him and then framed her face as he kissed her.

The kiss should have been fleeting. Instead, it went on for more than just a second, surprising them both. The depth, the feel and the emotion it dragged up certainly surprised Kane.

He had no idea what he might have been expecting from the impulsive contact, but he got a whole lot more than he might have ever bargained for. Instead of a simple release at best, the sudden, deep contact between them turned out to be something a great deal more. Something that came with its own promise of what was to come.

Before he knew it, his arms had gone around her and he was holding Kelly against him, melding her body to his as if they were destined to be fused.

For the first time in his life he felt as though he had touched hope, real hope. And for one shimmering moment in time, he felt whole.

Common sense demanded that he pull away. His inner needs, however, once roused, clamored for more time. More contact, more emotion.

More kissing.

More.

He broke contact, breathless and still very hungry for more, afraid of this persona within him that he didn't recognize or felt that he could completely control.

"Sorry," he apologized to Kelly, "I have no excuse

for my behavior except that it's just been one hell of an emotional time."

He couldn't be sorry about this. She wouldn't let him. An apology would blunt the magic of the moment.

"There's nothing to be sorry for. You just went on one hell of an emotional roller coaster. Went from thinking your uncle, your only family, was dead, to being told he might remain comatose for the rest of his life, to having him wake up, so to speak right before your eyes. You're entitled to be a little wobbly emotionally as well as physically."

Kane shook his head, marveling at the amount of words that could come pouring out of his partner. "You're hanging out your shingle again."

Okay, maybe she had gone a little overboard in her pep talk. But he mattered to her. And she was beginning to think it went far beyond just being his partner. Especially since she was still reeling internally from that lip-burning kiss he had planted on her.

"Sorry, guess you bring out the inner psychiatrist in me. I'll try to keep it under control." She glanced at the questionnaires on the side table. "Tell you what, after you go tell whoever needs to know about this new turn your uncle's taken, why don't we celebrate his return to consciousness by going over those questionnaires?" she suggested, knowing that Kane really needed a return to normalcy.

"Sure. Why not? Be right back," he promised as he went to fetch a nurse.

* * *

After a nurse as well as the doctor who had been summoned had come and gone, leaving a very hopeful prognosis in their wake, and Keith had once again drifted off to sleep, Kane got back down to business. He took a handful of questionnaires to review, leaving the last sheets for Kelly.

It took very little time for them to make note of the fact that all the victims had attended the same high school and that they all, at one point or another, had been on the school yearbook staff.

"It's our best lead so far," Kelly observed, doing her best to stifle yet another yawn that rose to her lips. It was getting to be a real losing battle.

Kane looked at her with what appeared to be concern. Except that, to the best of her knowledge, Kane never expressed concern.

"How much sleep have you gotten in the last couple of days?" Kane asked.

"Enough" was Kelly's automatic answer. She was actually fighting to keep her eyes open, but she wasn't about to admit it. Her needing a crutch—in this case, sleep—conflicted with her own self-image. "I just had a crazy idea."

"And this is different from all the other times, how?" Kane asked. Then, because she's stopped talking and was just glaring at him, Kane prompted her, "Sorry, couldn't resist. Go ahead."

She debated for a moment longer, then decided

this was for Aurora, to catch the thief and keep him from terrorizing another couple.

"You know how in all these movies they make about the nerdy kid in high school, he always finds a way to come back and get even with all the people who made his life so miserable during those teen years. It was always revenge they were after, giving those nasty people who made high school a living hell for them something to remember for the rest of their lives."

She could name half a dozen movies like that just off the top of her head. But she had a feeling that Kane hadn't a clue when it came to movies with that sort of scenario. The movies he watched probably had a lot of firepower in them and very little dialogue other than grunting and groaning.

"So, what exactly are you saying?" Kane asked, wanting her to pin it down for them.

"What if that's what we have here? What if all our victims picked on or were nasty to some very intelligent—albeit nerdy—student in high school? Did something to him that made him just want to die of embarrassment. An embarrassment that might still haunt him to this day, figuratively speaking, right? I think the guy is getting even because he's breaking into their homes and making them watch how he either steals or destroys their so-called treasures."

"Okay, let's say that you're right. Why now? Why not last year? Or two years ago?" Kane asked her.

Revenge was only half the story. What had been the trigger in this case?

"I'm working on that," Kelly answered, chewing on her bottom lip as she continued thinking.

He watched her for a moment, recalling just how those lips had felt like against his own. Chemistry had happened today.

That and admittedly a connection like he'd never felt before.

He saw her struggling to keep her eyes opened again. Okay, enough was enough.

"Think on it in the morning," he advised. "Right now, you're going home, to bed." It sounded more like an order than something being offered for consideration.

Kelly shook her head. "Too much work to do. Besides," she pointed out needlessly. "I'm keeping you company while you keep vigil."

"I'm going home, too," he told her. "Now that he's woken up and the doctors said that there's every chance he'll make a full recovery—especially if he starts his physical therapy regiment, which, thanks to you and the chief, looks like there's nothing to stop my uncle from making progress and then a full recovery.

"That means that I can go home and take a shower, as well as put on some fresh clothes."

"Okay, you talked me into it," she said, getting to her feet. Her balance was off and she found that she was just a little wobbly—and a lot more wobbly than she was happy about.

Her misstep almost had her colliding with Kane as he rose to his feet, as well. "Sorry," she murmured.

"That just proves my point," Kane declared.

Kelly cocked her head. This was going to be good. "Which is?"

"That you're too tired to drive yourself home safely."

She fought to keep her lids from drooping. "I'm fine."

"No, you're not and after all this I don't want to have to come back and keep vigil again, waiting for *you* to regain consciousness. Once is more than enough."

"I absolve you of that," she told him, stifling yet another yawn.

"That's not in your power," he informed her. "But it's in *my* power to drive you home."

He seemed to be forgetting about one thing. "What about my car?" she asked.

"It'll be here in the morning."

She knew that the city was relatively safe and the hospital parking lot even more so. Still, she didn't like the idea of leaving her car somewhere overnight.

"But—"

"Don't argue with me, Cavanaugh. I'm the lead detective, remember?"

"Not in all matters," she reminded him. "Just with this case."

"And while you're working the case, you're going to have to listen to me. I'm in charge of making the rules, Cavanaugh."

Kelly sighed as she rolled her eyes. "I'm too tired to argue."

If he had been a kid, he would have clapped his hands together. "I never thought I'd live to see the day you said that."

"In case you haven't noticed, there are a lot of miracles abounding today," she quipped, glancing over at his uncle.

When she looked back at Kane, she saw that he was regarding her intently. She couldn't begin to fathom what he was thinking.

"Yeah, there are," Kane said half under his breath.

"Don't get soft on me now, Durant. That alone would make me think that the Apocalypse is coming for us any day now."

"Coming? Hell, I'm looking right at it," Kane told her.

"Keep it down, you two. There's a man trying to sleep here," Keith pretended to grumble. The raspy voice was preceded by a racking cough.

"Sorry, Mr. Leeds, we'll get out of your hair," Kelly promised, pausing to bend down over the man and brush her lips against his cheek.

Kane heard his uncle sigh and saw him smile. Just

before he drifted off again, Keith said, "Don't mess up, kid. This one's a keeper."

Maybe you have something there, Keith, Kane thought as he ushered his partner out of the room.

"See you tomorrow," Kane said, raising his voice for his uncle hopefully to hear.

But Keith had already fallen asleep again, drifting off with a satisfied smile on his lips.

Chapter 16

"I'm really okay to drive," Kelly protested in the parking lot. "You don't have to go out of your way like this."

Kane unlocked the passenger side door and held it opened, looking at her expectantly. "Said the woman who hasn't slept for more than a couple of hours because she insisted on keeping her partner company as he kept vigil in the hospital." Kane all but ushered her into her seat, then pulled out the seat belt, turning the metal clasp over to her. "You didn't listen to me when I told you to go home."

With a sigh, she buckled herself in. "That's different."

"Why?" He rounded the hood and got in on the

driver's side. "Because you always get to have your way and I don't?"

What did that even mean? Kelly frowned. "You're confusing me."

"Another sign that you're punchy." Kane started up his car. Glancing into the rearview mirror, he pulled out of the parking spot. "The Kelly Cavanaugh that I know never gets confused—or at least would never admit that she was."

Kelly sighed and sank back into her seat as he drove on to the main thoroughfare. "Have it your way."

"Well, considering that you're in my car and it's in motion, I'll take a wild stab at it and say that I already am."

Kelly looked at his chiseled profile. He'd come a long way in the past few weeks. She was definitely having an effect on him. It seemed only fair, considering that he was affecting her.

"You know, you're doing an awful lot of talking for the strong, silent type."

She was right, and he knew the reason for that. In his relief and enthusiasm over his uncle's regaining consciousness, he'd slipped and kissed Kelly.

Big mistake.

That kiss that had been lingering on his mind ever since it happened. Kissing her had been a break in his self-restraint.

It had also, like it or not, opened up a whole new

world for him. A world he had never even given any thought to.

It wasn't a world he was comfortable in. Yet now that he had inadvertently entered it, he didn't really want to shut the door again—although that would have been the smarter way to go if all he was actually interested in was self-preservation.

He was interested in something more than just that. And it worried him.

A lot.

The traffic for once was sparse and he brought Kelly home pretty quickly. Rather than just letting her get out at the curb and walk to her front door, Kane got out, too. All he intended to do was walk her to her door, wait for her to unlock it and then go home from there. End of story. Or so he kept telling himself.

"You do know I'm a cop, right?" Kelly asked him, amused by this show of chivalry. "I can find my way to the front door."

Kane frowned. Maybe he should have his head examined after all for thinking what he was thinking, for being as damn attracted to this woman as he knew he was.

"My uncle would want me to do this."

"Oh, your uncle." There was just a touch of mockery in her voice, but on a whim, she played along.

"Okay, so if it was up to you, you'd what? Find a way to catapult me out of your sedan?"

He tried to envision that. "Might be worth considering," he countered. And then he broached what had been ricocheting around in his mind for hours now. "Look, about before."

"You might want to narrow that down," she suggested, pretending she didn't know *exactly* what he was referring to.

Putting what amounted to an apology into words was more than a little difficult for him. "I'm aware that it shouldn't have happened."

Kelly raised her eyes to his for a long moment. "Maybe it should have," she countered. Taking out her key, she held it in her hand for a second. "Do you want to come in?"

Yes, he did. Very, very much. Which was why he shouldn't, Kane told himself. "It's late."

"I didn't ask you for the time," she pointed out. "I asked you if you wanted to come inside."

"Yes, I would."

The second the words were out of his mouth, he knew he was going to regret them. But it was too late to take them back.

The smile that appeared on her face came in slow stages, like the unveiling of a new painting or the sunrise. She put the key into the lock and opened the door. Her fingers flew over the keypad as she rearmed her security system.

Kane watched her, surprised that she went to such lengths considering what she had said about the city and its diminishing crime rate.

"I thought you said this was a safe neighborhood," Kane challenged.

"It is." She saw no contradiction in what she said and what she did. "The security system is my concession to Seamus."

"Seamus," Kane repeated, leaning against the stucco wall. "I don't know who that is."

"Neither did I eighteen months ago," she admitted. She paused as she focused, wanting to get the lineage right. "Seamus was my grandfather's older brother. He and Andrew—Seamus's son—have this growing security systems business going. He was adamant about installing this system, not just in my house, but in my sisters' houses, as well. Apparently his motto is Better Safe than Sorry. Not exactly original," she admitted. "But his heart's in the right place."

From what he'd heard and gleaned, the family numbers had doubled with this last discovery. "Must get confusing," he mused. "Having all those brand-new Cavanaughs to keep track of."

Kelly suppressed a laugh. "Not so confusing. I'm getting the hang of it. To be honest, I have no idea what it feels like to have a small family. A crowd scene has always been the norm for me. Most of the time it's a comfortable feeling. If you fall, there's always someone to pick you up, dust you off, give you a pep talk and send you back in." She smiled at him, thinking how lonely his situation had to have been while growing up. "You can borrow any one of them anytime that you'd like."

Kane laughed. It was a crazy suggestion. "You mean like in a lending library?"

"In a way." Kicking off her shoes right beside the door, she turned around to face him. "Can I offer you something?"

His eyes met hers, telling her things that he felt he wasn't free to say out loud. Things he shouldn't even be thinking about. She was his partner, for God's sake. He needed to go before he did something he was going to wind up regretting.

Something he'd been wanting to do for a while now. "I think I'd better leave."

"If that's what you want…" Kelly's voice trailed off. The expression in her eyes, however, told him to stay.

"What I want?" It wasn't even remotely what he wanted. "No, but it's what I should do."

She disregarded his last sentence, focused instead on the feeling that was all but vibrating between them. "What do you want?" she asked in a soft, low voice that all but undulated along his skin. Making him feel hot.

"Kelly," he began, searching for the right words of protest that his conscience dictated he should utter.

She stopped him right there. "Right answer," she told him. Her smile was warm and inviting.

And he was a man who desperately needed to warm himself, to feel as if he was wanted. Still, he had to make sure she understood what was at stake. "Kelly, if I stay there's no turning back."

"Who says I want to turn back?" she asked, her lips flittering along his face, leaving small whispers of kisses to mark their passage.

Kane felt his gut tighten, felt a longing pervade his entire body. A body that was responding to her with mind-blowing speed.

"You should," he told her, his voice low.

"Convince me," she whispered, her very breath teasing him.

Undoing him.

Kane took her into his arms and kissed her. Kissed her as if his very existence depended on it. Kissed her as if this was the moment he was born for.

He didn't recognize himself. For as long as he could remember he had been restrained, his every move calculated, mentally rehearsed before it was ever executed. He'd never once just flown by the seat of his pants, not knowing what he was about to do until he was doing it.

But this—and this woman—demanded a whole different frame of reference, different parameters than anything he was accustomed to, anything he'd ever done before.

The way she responded, the way she made him feel, the way her mouth moved both beneath his and along his skin, just set him on fire. Made him want with such intensity that everything except for her became a blur. She was his beginning, his middle and, most likely, his end.

And he didn't care.

Didn't care that he wasn't the one calling the shots, didn't care that at this very moment he was a virtual prisoner of these very demanding needs. As long as she was in his arms, that was all that mattered.

Pandora's box.

That was what she'd opened, Kelly realized. And instead of demons, as the old fable went, what she had wound up releasing was a whole different side of herself. A side that she had never suspected existed.

Her heart was pounding and she felt almost primitive in her needs, her desires. It didn't matter. All that mattered was this moment, this man.

Clothes went flying.

It wasn't an orderly process, one garment at a time with each of them moving tantalizingly slow. It was more of an immediate response. Clothing was in the way, so it was ripped aside.

The need to touch and be touched all but overwhelmed her.

And the moment he did touch her, the moment he

passed his hands possessively over her, Kelly felt an inner explosion, the first of several that would follow, each astonishingly greater than the last.

Her head began to reel.

Biting back a moan, Kelly struggled to give as good as she got, to make him as much her prisoner as she was his.

The thrill of his hard body moving along hers, teasing her, tantalizing her, driving her crazy, almost drove her over the edge, but she managed to hold that last little bit of her in check until she was certain he was primed and ready and unable to keep from taking her any longer.

They were a tangle of limbs, somehow moving from the sofa—when had they reached that?—onto the floor.

Each movement, each new angle, was marked by myriad passionate kisses, all played against a backdrop of pounding hearts and racing pulses.

She arched against him as he kissed the hollow of her throat, worked his way down to her breasts, her quivering belly and then to the very core of her. A cry of sheer ecstasy escaped her lips before she could press them closed. Before she even knew what was happening.

It only seemed to incite him further.

And then, as they both grappled with the fringes of exhaustion, Kane drew his body over hers. Their eyes met and held.

Her adrenaline reached an all-time high.

The next moment Kane entered her and the last bastion was breached. The inner rhythm that ensued found them both, urged them on up to the final pinnacle.

Fireworks went off, touching the sky before raining down on her, and from the way she heard Kane breathing heavily, she had not been the only one caught in the shower.

She felt Kane's muscular arms tighten around her as the last sensation seized him in its grip before retreating.

Kane's heart pounded against hers, pounded so hard until every drop of energy left her body. Kelly closed her arms around him, absorbing him, loving him.

Scaring herself. But in a good way, she couldn't help thinking, trying not to panic.

"So what else can I get you?" Kelly whispered against his ear.

Kane pushed himself up with his hands, feeling as if this was some sort of a strangely erotic push-up. He looked at her incredulously. His serious face dissolved as laughter progressively grew louder and overtook him.

Deep, resonant and heartfelt, his laughter was infectious. Within a second, Kelly was laughing, too, until they were both wrapped up in it, in the sound and the feeling.

Rolling off her, Kane pulled her to him, unwilling to give up this unusual closeness he was experiencing just yet.

"I didn't mean for that to happen, you know," he told her.

Her eyes were dancing with mischief as she released a heartfelt sigh.

"If that's what happens when you *don't* mean it, warn me when you do mean it, because I'll have to get my affairs in order." Turning toward him, she saw the puzzled expression on Kane's face. Without waiting for him to ask, she explained, "Because there's no way I could survive anything of even a tiny bit larger magnitude than this. Actually, I barely survived this." Propping herself up on her elbow, she watched him, her smile growing deeper and larger. Against all reason, she asked, "Wanna do it again?"

"You're kidding," Kane breathed. What was the woman made of?

"Wouldn't there be laughter if I were kidding? I don't hear any," she told him. "Do you?"

Kane laughed then, softly, to himself as he shook his head. "You are really something else, Kelly. Give me a minute—no, make that five." For reasons he couldn't fully understand, he was beyond secrets, beyond embarrassment. That was the only reason he admitted, "You sapped all my energy."

"Tell you what. I'm feeling generous. I'll give you

ten, as long as you go on holding me like this until you're ready."

She felt his smile against her cheek. Another wave of warmth unfurled within her. "You drive a hard bargain, but I think I can handle it."

Kelly curled her body into his, thinking how right that felt. And trying to fathom why that felt scary, as well.

"I think you can handle anything that's thrown at you," Kelly said.

Except for you, he thought.

Kane toyed with her hair, wrapped a strand around his finger. There was something comforting about its silky feel against his flesh. "I'm not nearly as confident about that as you are."

"You could have fooled me," she told him.

Resting her head on his chest, she slowly traced small, concentric circles along his skin, allowing only her fingertips to graze his body lightly.

The lighter her touch, Kane realized, the more he responded—until all of him felt almost as hard as a rock. Certainly ready to go on another wild, exhilarating roller-coaster ride.

There were rules against this sort of thing happening. Department rules and, more importantly to Kane, his own rules. But being with Kelly like this, lost in intimacy, somehow made breaking all the rules the right thing to do.

He had to be out of his mind. There was no other explanation for it.

But that—and the rest of it—were things he would reexamine and deal with later.

Much later.

In the morning.

Right now his attention was focused on something entirely different. Something far more urgent than guilt or penance or confusion.

He wanted to make love with her again.

Pressing a kiss to her temple, he said, "I think I'm ready now."

Her smile, so angelic before, was positively wicked now as she raised herself up ever so slightly, her eyes washing over him.

"I think you are, too."

Chapter 17

His house was just as nice.

Nicer.

Definitely warmer looking and not nearly so blatantly ostentatious.

His mouth curved as he shook his head. There was no humor in his smile, he knew. The oversize house reflected the couple who lived inside it. It all but shouted: Hey, look at me. I'm rich and you're not.

Twenty years and nothing had changed.

He'd harbored a hope that it had. But then, he supposed that despite his vast technical background, he'd always been a dreamer. Always hoped that tomorrow would be better than today. Hoped that once they all got together, there would be apologies. That was all he'd really wanted, an apology for their treatment of him in the past. Once he heard it, he could move forward, could forgive and could attempt to forget.

But there were no apologies. Not a single one. All he saw were the same sneering, condescending looks that had haunted him all those years ago. Back then, he'd used the humiliations to fire up his determination, to do what he'd had to do to become a respected man in his field.

To open doors that hadn't been opened before.

Ironically, the condescension he'd encountered had made him strong, made him determined to be successful and make something of himself. He wound up building the software company he now helmed. Wound up being a respected man in his field. He'd done it all in the hope that the people who had belittled him, laughed at him, shunned him would realize how wrong they'd been to treat him that way. All in the hope they would attempt to make amends.

But that dream had crashed and burned five weeks ago. Nothing had changed. If anything, it had grown more intense.

He'd told himself that they were just jealous that he had made such strides, accomplished so much while they had done nothing more than aged.

But knowing that wasn't enough. Not nearly enough.

He'd have no peace until he made them pay for what they had done. That meant hitting them where they lived. That meant taking from them that which they valued the most. Their possessions and their pride.

He couldn't go home until he had the satisfaction of knowing he'd made them pay for all the countless humiliations, large and small, he'd been forced to suffer in those four long years so long ago.

He wouldn't be able to live with himself if he allowed this last opportunity to just slip through his fingers. Those narcissistic bastards would never know what—or who—had hit them. But whether they knew or not didn't matter. *He'd* know, and, in the long run, that was all that really mattered.

He'd been sitting out here since the sun had gone down. By his watch, he had another two hours to go. He wanted them asleep, too groggy to put up a fight until it was too late.

He was systematically going down the line, dealing with one jackass at a time, and he was almost finished. Just a few more pompous idiots to take down and he would be done.

Just a few more.

He glanced at his watch again and shifted in the car.

Just a few more, he silently repeated.

And that was worth waiting for.

She had always been a light sleeper. So when Kane attempted to quietly leave her bed hours later and get dressed, his effort was doomed from the start.

Kelly felt him stirring.

Opening her eyes, she saw that Kane already had managed to pull on his jeans. His shirt and shoes were in his hands and he was trying to tiptoe out of the room.

"You don't have to go, you know."

Turning around, he told her, "I didn't mean to wake you."

"It's okay. But I meant what I just said. You don't have to go."

Kelly sat up, her hair cascading down around her bare shoulders. She looked, he couldn't help thinking as desire overtook him, like some sort of a goddess—as well as his complete undoing.

Kelly tucked the sheet around herself, but her eyes never left his.

"Don't worry, I'm not going to make you take me to the senior prom. And I'm not going to make an announcement to the world at large that we're going steady. We're both adults and we just enjoyed one another's company. No big deal," she told him, trying to keep her voice as light as possible because, to her, it really *was* a big deal.

But she intended to keep that to herself.

"Maybe it was a big deal," he contradicted. Because she gave him so much space, he found himself wanting to decrease it.

"Maybe it was," she agreed softly. Her eyes held his. His expression was impossible to read, but she went with her gut—and hoped ultimately she wasn't going to regret it.

Less than a heartbeat before he leaned in to kiss her, their cell phones went off, ringing almost in harmony.

Kelly groaned. "Talk about bad timing…"

"The call—or us?" Kane asked.

The wicked look in her eyes was back. "I'll leave that for you to figure out. Okay, okay," she cried, addressing the last words to her phone. "I'm coming."

It took a couple of minutes, but she managed to locate her phone beneath the pile of the clothing they'd shed much earlier. She picked it up. "Cavanaugh," she said as she braced herself.

Kane already had found his cell phone and was talking to the person who had called him at what some might have considered an ungodly hour. But then, criminals didn't keep regular hours.

For purposes of mental clarity, Kane knew he should have looked away from Kelly, who was on her cell talking to someone while she climbed back into bed, completely and unselfconsciously nude.

He felt his palms grow itchy, felt desire well up within him with a vengeance. He wanted her—and that was a bad sign.

Almost in self-defense, he turned away so that he actually could concentrate on what the person on the other end of the call was telling him.

Turning back around, he saw that Kelly's call had

already terminated and she was standing, dressed and ready to go. The woman was a regular whirl-wind.

"That was fast," he commented.

Her grin was almost impish, giving him a glimpse of what she must have been like as a girl. "I was one of seven and I grew up in a house with two bathrooms. Eventually, Dad had a third one put in, but because there were only two to begin with, I learned how to get ready really, really fast or risk having one of my brothers come barging in on me if I took too long." She nodded at the cell he was still holding. "I take it that you got the same call I did."

It seemed a safe enough assumption. "There's been another identical home invasion."

"Not so identical," she contradicted as they went down the stairs and to the front door. "This time one of the home owners fought back and wound up having to be taken to the hospital."

"Sounds like the thief is upping his game," Kane commented.

"Or had it upped for him," she suggested. After swiftly arming her security system, she closed the front door and hurried to Kane's car.

"How do you mean?" Kane asked.

"Sounds like the home owner either rushed our guy, or the home owner got loose and decided to fight back. Either way, there was a physical altercation. I have a feeling that the thief might have panicked."

"Sounds like a possibility," Kane agreed. "With luck we'll know more once we question the home owners."

"*If* we can question them," she qualified.

Driving to one of the main thoroughfares, Kane gave her a quizzical look. "What do you mean? Why wouldn't we be able to question them?"

"According to dispatch, when the owner fought back, the thief just started swinging, wound up shoving the owner. The guy stumbled backward, fell and hit his head on his marble coffee table. When the EMTs arrived, they found the victim unconscious and unresponsive."

Kane's frown deepened as he shook his head. "This is just sounding better and better," he murmured under his breath.

Pressing down on the accelerator, he picked up speed. With little traffic at that time of night—or morning, depending on one's point of view—they managed to make excellent time.

They arrived at the hospital within a few minutes. Because he was still unconscious when he had been brought in, the latest home invasion victim, Matthew Wallace, had been admitted to the hospital proper for extended observation.

Starting at the ER, Kane and she located the nurse who had ministered to Wallace's wounds. "You just missed him," the nurse told them. "They took him up to room 512. Take the tower elevators. They'll get you there quickly."

They followed the signs on wall. After a couple of twists and turns, Kane found the tower elevators.

"Maybe I should be dropping bread crumbs," Kelly said.

"I've got a pretty decent sense of direction," Kane told her. "I'll get us back."

She grinned as they got on the elevator. "Knew you were good for something," she teased.

Kane merely smiled that half smile of his.

They were communicating, Kelly thought, pleased at the way things were going.

When the elevator doors opened again, they stepped out on the fifth floor. Wallace's room was directly across from the nurse's station.

The unconscious man's wife was with him. Looking quite the worse for wear, Jill Wallace was pacing the room, wringing her hands and obviously having a very difficult time calming down her nerves. She stifled a scream when he and Kelly entered the room.

"Mrs. Wallace?" Kane asked politely.

"And if I am?" Jill Wallace's hazel eyes darted back and forth between them as if she was afraid if she looked away, one of them might try to harm her.

"We're with the Aurora PD. Detectives Cavanaugh," he nodded toward Kelly, "and Durant." They held out their respective IDs. Jill Wallace took an extra long time staring at them. "Would you mind telling us exactly what happened?"

"That—that *nerd*," Mrs. Wallace uttered the word as if it was a curse, "tried to rob us. He came into our bedroom and had the nerve to wake us up. He held a gun on us and made me tie Matthew up. Then he tied my hands together really tightly."

She pressed her lips together to keep from giving way to tears. "I was afraid he was going to—you know—assault me. But all he wanted to do was make us watch as he slashed that awful painting Matthew insisted on buying when we were in Holland."

Something had caught Kelly's attention right from the start. "You called the thief a nerd," Kelly said.

Mrs. Wallace blinked, as if she couldn't understand why that would bother the detective. "What about it?"

"Why would you do that?" Kelly asked, slowly working her way to her real question.

"Because he was," the woman insisted angrily. "He was one then, and he's still one now."

Kane exchanged a pointed look with her. Could they have finally caught a break? "You *recognized* him?" he asked the older woman.

"Well, yes, of course I did." She said it as if she was talking to mentally impaired people.

"How?" Kelly asked. "Was it something about his voice or the way he was standing or—"

"It was his face," Mrs. Wallace's tone was condescending. "His *face* was what gave him away." She rolled her eyes impatiently, as if applying to a higher power for patience.

"You actually *saw* his face?" Kane asked.

The woman's impatience grew. "Of course I saw his face. Aren't you people listening? No wonder we're at the mercy of larcenous nerds if you're the best that—"

Kane pushed aside the flash of temper he felt over the woman's condescending attitude toward Kelly. He needed to be perfectly clear about what the woman was telling him. "Wait. He wasn't wearing a mask?" That didn't make any sense, Kane thought. In all the other home invasions the thief had been dressed in black and worn a ski mask over his face. Why would the MO change now?

Mrs. Wallace sighed dramatically. She looked around as if addressing some invisible audience of on-lookers. "Why can't they let you smoke in their lousy hospital rooms?" She turned again to face both of them. "Yes, he was wearing a mask, but when Matthew got loose he pulled Howard's mask off, exposing him."

"Howard," Kane repeated, waiting for the woman to give him a last name.

"Yes. Howard Anderson. What's wrong with you? Can't you people keep up?" she demanded impatiently.

The name the woman mentioned was familiar to Kelly only because she had gone over the high school yearbook. "Howard Anderson was one of the names

I saw listed under the school yearbook staff. He went to school with you," she said to Jill.

"Oh, please, don't get me started." Jill rolled her eyes again. "That loser was pathetic then and he's just as pathetic now."

The woman seemed to have a great deal of contempt for a man who had been clever enough to bypass a variety of different security systems and catch all his victims off guard.

"What can you tell us about Howard?" Kelly asked the woman, wanting to get a more complete picture of the man who had just become their lead suspect. "What was he like in high school?"

The woman sneered haughtily. "I told you. Pathetic. He used to follow us around like some kind of a lost puppy dog. The guys used to make him run errands and give him things to do just to see how far they could push him." Her laugh was cruel, Kelly couldn't help thinking.

"It was all pretty funny. Howard was so eager to please, so desperate to be accepted," Jill Wallace said, her voice dripping with scorn. "As if he was ever going to be equal to any of us." Jill shook her head as memories apparently came back to her. "They gave him outlandish things to do—and the jerk always did them."

"Did this go on all through high school?" Kelly asked. Always on the side of the underdog, she felt her heart go out to Howard Anderson. He must have gone through a hellish four years.

"Yes." And then Jill reconsidered. "Well, until Matthew and some of the other guys decided to steal Howard's clothes while he was in the shower after gym class. They ran his clothes up a flagpole and he had no choice but to climb up there, naked." She paused to shiver. "He had such a pathetically thin body," she recalled with utter disdain. "And he got his clothes."

"Where were the teachers?" Kelly demanded, sickened by what the woman was saying. Even more sickened by the fact that the woman seemed to regard the awful incident as humorous rather than utterly offensive.

Jill's shoulders rose and fell indifferently. "I don't know. Watching from the sidelines, probably. Howard stopped following the guys around after that. He finally learned his place. We didn't see him until the reunion."

"The reunion?" Kane questioned.

"Our twenty-year high school reunion," Jill stressed haughtily, as if any idiot with even a double digit IQ would know that. "Howard had the nerve to show up and try to impress us with some stupid computer software he developed. Once a nerd, always a nerd," she said dismissively. "Matthew shot him down pretty fast, asking when he intended to stop playing games and get a real job."

She paused to look over toward her unconscious

husband. "Howard should be put away for life for hurting Matthew the way he did."

Kane didn't bother to point out that the penalty was too great to fit the crime—and that Matthew apparently provoked the suspect, perhaps even reverting back to his high school big-man-on-campus persona, jeering at the man he perceived to be beneath him.

"Out of sheer curiosity, Mrs. Wallace, who took the first swing tonight?" Kelly asked.

The woman lifted her head proudly. "Why, Matthew did. The second we saw who it was. Of course, I helped," she added quickly. "If it wasn't for me, Matthew wouldn't have been able to get free. I didn't tie his wrists up tightly the way Anderson wanted me to." She tossed her hair. "I wanted Matthew to get loose and rescue me." She pursed her lips together in a reproving frown. "If the idiot hadn't tripped backward and hit that thick skull of his, he would have pulverized Howard." Her eyes were blazing now as she looked from Kane to his partner. "Are you going to go get him?" she demanded again. "Or do you get paid just to stand around?"

Kelly banked down the strong urge to strangle the woman. "We're definitely going to look for him. You wouldn't know where he lived, would you?" Kelly asked her.

"Why would I know something like that?" Mrs. Wallace asked haughtily. But the next moment she shrugged indifferently and said, "It's Seattle, I think. I think I overheard Anderson saying that he only came back to Aurora for the reunion."

"And when, exactly, did that reunion take place?" Kelly asked.

Mrs. Wallace thought for a minute. "It was almost five weeks ago. Why?" she asked. "Is that important?"

"It might be," Kane replied in a tone that clearly stated the time for talk was over.

"Five weeks," Kelly said later as they left the hospital. There was excitement in her voice as she reminded her partner, "That's when the home invasions started." Her smile could have melted a ten-foot snowdrift, its wattage was that intense. "That's our connection."

Kane nodded. "When Anderson saw that he was still the odd man out no matter what his accomplishments, that most likely was the trigger that set him off, and he decided to get revenge on these people who made him such a laughingstock."

They were driving back to the precinct to do a little research before hitting the streets again. It was still dark outside and the moonlight created rainbows in the occasional oil slick on the ground.

Kelly took it all in, thinking. She couldn't help but feel sorry for the man they were pursuing.

"I know he broke the law and all," she began,

"but to be honest, after dealing with these vapid, self-involved narcissists, I can't blame him for what he did. As a matter of fact, I applaud him for his restraint. I would have been tempted to pound on each of them."

"Yeah, you would, wouldn't you?" Kane laughed. "Anderson got even with them by hitting them where it hurt. In their pockets. I agree with you that they had it coming, but, justified or not, that's not our decision to make. We're still going to have to bring Anderson in for questioning if nothing else."

Kelly nodded, resigned. "I know, I know. But I don't have to like it."

After stopping at a red light, he looked at her for a long moment. "You know, I never suspected that you were a pushover." What he didn't say was that he found this side of her incredibly appealing.

Kelly frowned at his assessment. "I'm not a pushover. I just sympathize with the underdog, that's all." She redirected the conversation. "Mrs. Wallace said that Anderson lived in Seattle now. We could start looking for him there."

Kane shook his head. "I doubt that he's commuting from Seattle just to pull off these home invasions. The reunion was five weeks ago. He probably rented a hotel room when he first came out. What if when he decided to make these people pay for their horrible treatment of him, he just extended his stay?

That seems like a simple way to go from where I'm sitting."

"Sounds like a definite possibility," Kelly agreed. This was nice, she thought. They were operating like a team rather than sparring over every little thing. She liked this approach a great deal more than the way things had previously been between them. "Why don't I have my sister pull up Anderson's credit cards and see if there's been any recent activity and, if so, where. That'll narrow down the playing field for us."

Kane nodded as they drew closer to the precinct. "Good idea."

Kelly inclined her head and pretended to be like some of the home invasion victims they had previously interviewed. "Yes, I know," she said with an affected haughtiness.

"Your cleverness is only exceeded by your modesty," Kane observed, playing along.

"I know that, too." And then Kelly dropped the attitude. "While Valri is researching his card activity, we could try showing Anderson's picture to our other home invasion victims, see if they remember him with the fondness that Mrs. Wallace does."

"Looks like, with any luck, we're finally going to be wrapping this one up," Kane told her, allowing just a sliver of optimism to rise to the surface.

Kelly nodded. But even so, she couldn't help wondering if by wrapping up this case, they would be

wrapping up whatever it was that was going on between them, as well.

That she *didn't* want happening, she realized with
the suddenness of an awakening. Whatever *was*
going on between them, she wanted it to continue,
to take root and assume some sort of recognizable,
permanent shape. *Then* they could decide whether
or not they were in for the long haul.

Although, she suspected she already knew what
her own answer to that would be.

It turned out to be a relatively easy matter for
Valri to track down Howard Anderson's recent credit
card activity. The gaming genius—as Valri referred
to Anderson—had made no effort to hide anything.
It seemed, Valri told her sister, that Anderson either
didn't care if he was discovered or he was that con-
temptuous of the authorities' ability to track him down.

"Looks like you were right," Kelly told Kane.
"Anderson is still staying in the same hotel suite he
reserved when he attended the reunion."

This was almost too easy, Kelly thought as she
and Kane drove to the Ambassador Hotel to take
Anderson into custody for questioning.

"He wants to be found," she told Kane.

Was that it? Did the man want what he probably
regarded as long overdue recognition of his mental
superiority over the people who had undoubtedly
made his life a living hell in high school? It had a

fatalistic ring to it, she couldn't help thinking. There had to be another answer.

"I wouldn't go that far," Kane told her.

"I would," Kelly countered, pushing the envelope a little further. "Anderson knows that what he did was wrong, no matter how provoked he was. Someone as smart as he is would have tried to hide his trail. Yet, he didn't. Why not? Why didn't he try to hide his trail?"

"If he's as big a deal as your sister seems to think he is, then what those self-absorbed people said or did should have just rolled off Anderson's back."

Kelly had a different opinion on that score. "Should have," she allowed. "But didn't. Inside, we're all just the same vulnerable, insecure kids we were when we were growing up."

Something in Kelly's voice caught his attention. Was she talking about herself, he wondered, or was she saying something entirely different?

He looked at her intently as he asked, "Speaking from experience?"

"Speaking from empathy," Kelly corrected. And then she let the subject drop. "Which room number did they say that Anderson was in?"

"Suite 1018," Kane answered.

They made their way to the tenth floor.

There was no response when they knocked on the

hotel suite door, nor did anyone answer when Kane called out to Anderson through the door.

"We should have brought the hotel manager with us to unlock the door." That had been an oversight on his part, Kane upbraided himself.

Turning on his heel, Kane began to head back to the elevator. But he stopped when he realized that Kelly wasn't right beside him or even behind him. He turned around to find that she hadn't budged from the suite's door.

"Kelly?"

"Hang on." Kelly tossed the words over her shoulder as she focused on the business at hand.

Kane retraced his steps back to her.

Kelly was working the lock, he realized. She had two thin metal tools in her hands, both of which were inserted into the lock.

Burglar tools? Kane wondered. There had to be another explanation.

"What are you doing?" he asked.

"Putting some of my unorthodox education to use," she replied. Then she explained, "Brennan taught me this. It's a little trick he picked up while undercover with the DEA." And then her look of deep concentration vanished. "Ah," she grunted triumphantly. "Voilà."

After slowly turning the knob, she opened the door.

The exclamation "ta-da!" froze on her tongue.

It froze because the first thing she saw was Howard Anderson, hanging from a chandelier.

Chapter 18

"Omigod!" Kelly cried as she and Kane ran into the hotel room.

Kane quickly righted the fallen chair that was beneath Anderson's body. It wasn't hard to surmise its previous use. Jumping on it, Kane wrapped his arms around the unconscious smaller man and held him up so that the noose around his neck was no longer pulled tight, stealing his very life away.

"Find something to cut the rope with, Cavanaugh! I can't hold him like this for long," Kane shouted.

Kelly looked around, but she didn't see anything that could be used to cut through the rope. So instead she dragged another chair over to the one that Kane was standing on. Climbing up onto the seat, she raised herself on her toes as far as she could and began to work at the knot to loosen the noose.

It turned out to be far more difficult than she thought.

"Work faster, Kelly. He's getting heavier and I don't know how much longer I can hold him," Kane warned urgently.

"I'm trying, I'm trying," she cried, frustrated with the process. "This guy had to be an Eagle Scout at one point. I've never seen knots like this before," she complained. And then another worry hit her. "Is he breathing?"

"Doesn't feel like it. I can't exactly check his pulse right now," Kane pointed out.

Kelly blew out a triumphant breath. "Got it!" she exclaimed.

Working fast she widened the noose and removed it from around the man's neck. She worked the rope up over Anderson's head and then just let go of the noose. With nothing to anchor it in place, it swung eerily back and forth, empty now. A symbol of cheated death.

No longer needing to keep Anderson elevated, Kane lowered his arms and allowed the man's head to drop against his shoulder.

Working with Kelly, who was still standing on the chair, Kane got Anderson down onto the floor and tried to detect the man's pulse.

"Anything?" Kelly cried anxiously.

Kane didn't answer her immediately, not until he was sure. "I think so—yes," he confirmed. "It's faint, but it's still there." Still squatting over Anderson, Kane rocked back on his heels. "Looks like we came in just after he kicked the chair out from under himself. Call for a bus, Kelly," he instructed and began performing CPR.

She rode in the ambulance with Anderson while Kane followed behind in his car. Eventually, they were going to need a car to drive back to the precinct. Otherwise, he would have ridden in the ambulance along with Kelly and the unconscious suspect.

To his relief, Kane had managed to get the man breathing again just as the paramedics arrived. He'd stepped back to allow them to take over.

Although he was now breathing on his own, Anderson remained unconscious and unresponsive.

She would have to wait to get answers to the questions that filled her head, Kelly thought impatiently. Questions that went beyond the clichéd: "Did you really think you were going to get away with it?"

Over the course of their investigation, she had found herself growing to dislike the so-called victims, and now that they apparently had the man responsible for the home invasions in custody, she totally sympathized with him. Being an outsider who desperately wanted to belong the way that Anderson had during those years, had to have been brutal.

Especially during high school when insecurities ran rampant and egos fed on the destroyed self-esteem of others.

It was obvious that Anderson had been put through hell and still had kept coming back for more, praying the worst was over.

Except that it never was.

She couldn't excuse what the software genius ultimately had done, but she definitely could understand why he had done it.

In his place, who knew, she might have done the same thing, Kelly thought, studying the unconscious man strapped to the gurney.

Kane was less than a minute behind the ambulance. When it arrived at the hospital, he parked almost right next to it.

The paramedics disembarked and took possession of the gurney, bringing Anderson through the ER entrance. Kane caught Kelly by the arm, stopping her from following the man into the exam room.

He could see by the expression on her face where her sympathies were. The woman was definitely too softhearted for her own good. But at the same time, it made her appealingly human.

"Anything?" Kane asked, releasing her arm.

Kelly shook her head. "He didn't regain consciousness," she told him. "Considering what's waiting for him once he wakes up, remaining unconscious might be the better way for him to go. At least for a while."

Kane looked at the wide double doors the paramedics had gone through with Anderson. "Why do you think he wanted to kill himself?"

"My first thought is that he probably believed that he killed the last guy and was consumed with guilt." She looked toward the closed doors, as if she could see Anderson if she concentrated hard enough. "Murder was never on his agenda."

"How can you be so sure?" Kane questioned.

"I just am," she replied with conviction. "Anderson wanted to humiliate these people who made his life a living hell, not kill them."

"And you know this because?" Kane asked her.

This, for once, was simplicity on a half shell. "Because if they're dead, their humiliation is effectively at an end, and Anderson wants those people who tortured him in high school to suffer as much as he did."

They were currently standing right outside of the ER examination room, waiting for a prognosis from the attending physician. They also were waiting for permission to talk to Anderson the second the man regained consciousness.

Kelly frowned, looking through the upper portion of the swinging doors. It was made of glass, and she had a clear view of what was happening in the next room.

An ER physician as well as several nurses were

all working over Anderson. So far it didn't appear as if the man was responding.

"I almost wish we didn't have to arrest him," Kelly murmured.

Kane looked at her for a long moment, but his thoughts had nothing to do with the man beyond the swinging double doors. Instead, he was thinking how far he and the woman he'd been partnered with had come in such a short amount of time. It all but took his breath away. Something like this had never happened to him before. He'd never felt the kind of connection to another human being—other than his uncle—that he felt with her. He hadn't allowed it.

But this time, allowed or not, it made no difference. She had come on like gangbusters, breeching the wall he'd always kept in place around himself and crumbling it as if it was just so much powdered sugar.

He wondered what Kelly would say if she knew what he was thinking right this moment. Would she smile triumphantly—or run for the hills?

"You getting soft on me, Cavanaugh?" he asked her, doing his best to stick to the subject at hand.

"I've always been soft," she informed him. "I just pretend to have a crusty exterior. Keeps people from pushing me around." She looked at Kane. "Do you think if we put in a good word for him, whoever winds up prosecuting the case will go easy on Anderson?"

Something in her tone, something about what

she'd just said about keeping people from pushing her around, gave him pause.

"Do you identify with him?" Kane asked incredulously. In his eyes, the two couldn't have been more different, but that was just his take on the matter. Maybe he was missing a piece of the puzzle.

It was a yes-and-no situation. She tempered her answer to indicate that. "Not completely. I've always had people sticking up for me until I could do it myself." She looked through the glass again at Anderson. "Still, there but for the grace of God... You know the rest." And then she shook off her somber mood and smiled at Kane. "I already told you, I identify with the underdog."

The next moment, Kane tapped her arm to redirect her attention. The attending ER physician, a tall, authoritative-looking doctor by the name of Walter Manheim, was coming toward them.

"How is he?" Kane asked the gray-haired man

"Lucky," the doctor answered with feeling. "If you hadn't gotten there when you did, he'd be in the morgue right now rather than on his way to recovery."

"Has he regained consciousness at all?" Kelly asked.

To her surprise, the doctor nodded. "In the last five minutes—but just barely."

"Can we talk to him?" Kane asked.

Dr. Manheim took a deep breath, as if that would help him decide what was best for the patient. Finally, he nodded. "Just don't stay too long," he cautioned. "The man is very weak, and he needs his rest."

Kane was already on his way, but Kelly hung back. She had another question for the attending physician. "There was a man brought in by ambulance earlier today. He had a head trauma," she specified. "Can you tell me what his prognosis is? It's all part of the same case," she interjected before Dr. Manheim could protest that he wasn't able to discuss another patient.

The doctor nodded. Apparently, he was familiar with the case she was asking about. "Turned out that there was no internal swelling of the brain. The man was just knocked out. There's every indication that he's going to make a full recovery."

"One less thing to worry about," Kelly told her partner, who had retraced his steps when he saw that she was still talking to the ER doctor.

"At least they won't be charging him with second-degree murder," Kane commented as they went in to see the man whose life they had saved.

Howard Anderson's eyelids were just fluttering open when they walked into the room.

"I'm not dead, am I?" Anderson asked weakly when he saw them. There was a touch of resigned hopelessness in his voice.

"Doesn't look that way," Kane replied, reverting to the monotone voice he used when questioning suspects.

"Can't even die successfully," Anderson lamented

in pure disgust. Tears shone in his eyes as he stared up at the ceiling. It was obvious that he was struggling not to cry.

"Oh, you were definitely on the right road," Kelly told him. "If Detective Durant hadn't found you when he did and held you up so someone else could get the noose off your neck, you would have become just another suicide statistic." Out of the corner of her eye, she saw Kane glare at her, but she pretended not to notice. Instead, she continued to focus on Anderson. "Why did you try to kill yourself?" she asked.

"Because I killed Matthew!" Anderson cried. There was a hitch in his voice. "You have to believe me. I didn't mean for that to happen." He was pleading for their understanding, even though his voice was filled with self-loathing. "He grabbed me and I guess I freaked out. For a second I was back in the gym locker room in high school." He shivered at the memory. "I just pushed back with all my might." Anderson let out a shaky breath, looking as if he was reliving an ordeal. "When it happened the last time, I swore I'd never let one of them ever lay a hand on me again. But now Matthew's dead and it's all my fault." Before he turned his head away Kelly thought she glimpsed tears sliding down the man's cheek.

"You said you swore you'd never let one of them ever lay a hand on you *again*. They did before?" Kelly questioned. She was already aware of the story, thanks to Jill Wallace, but she wanted to hear Anderson's side of it.

Anderson's face turned a bright shade of red out of pure embarrassment. But then he shrugged, as if nothing mattered any more. Not dark secrets and certainly not pride.

"Back in high school. A bunch of the jocks stole all my clothes, tied them to a flagpole line and ran them straight up the flagpole. They told me if I wanted them I'd have to climb up the pole, naked, to get them. When I started to go up, they took turns swatting my butt like I was some kind of an animal who moved faster when whacked…" His voice caught and then just trailed off.

Kelly couldn't stand it. Anderson looked wretched and tortured. "He's not dead," she told him.

Anderson turned his face in her direction, his eyes listless. "Who?"

"Matthew Wallace. He's not dead," she repeated.

His face suddenly came alive. "What? I saw him. He hit his head on that ugly marble coffee table and then went down like a stone."

"The stone bounced," Kane remarked, taking pity on the man, as well. "You didn't kill anybody."

There was a hitch in Anderson's voice, this time forged by pure relief. "Oh, thank God!" he cried. And then, as the gravity of the situation hit him again, he sobered. "What's going to happen now?"

"You'll have to be arraigned and charged with

several counts of robbery," Kane told him. "Do you have a lawyer?"

Anderson nodded. Rather than concerned, he still appeared exceedingly relieved. "He's the best around."

"Good," Kane responded. "I'd say that you're going to need him."

"But you're sure that Matthew's alive?" Anderson asked again.

"Absolutely," Kelly replied. "He'll probably be discharged before you are."

The sigh that escaped Anderson's lips was one of utter relief.

"How do you think it'll go for him?" Kelly asked as she and Kane left the ER and walked to the front of the hospital.

"It's hard to say, but if his lawyer gets those so-called victims on the stand and they start running their mouths off, I'd say they'll be lucky if the jury doesn't recommend putting *them* in jail and letting Anderson go free." He stopped walking. Something had been bothering him for a while now. "Why did you tell Anderson that I was the one who saved his life?"

"Because you did," she replied, looking, he couldn't help thinking, incredibly wide-eyed and innocent. And absolutely damn sexy. It took all he had not to pull her into his arms and kiss her.

She had managed to trigger a side of him that he'd

never even suspected existed—and he had to admit that he rather liked it.

"Not alone," he pointed out. "You were the one who got the noose off his neck. I couldn't have done it on my own."

She shrugged. "It sounded more dramatic with just you being the hero. Besides, I thought you could do with a little gratitude sent your way. Given the man's ever-growing company, you'll probably be the recipient of an endless stream of video games for the rest of your natural life."

A less than overjoyed look entered Kane's eyes. "Video games," he repeated.

Kelly nodded. "For the rest of your natural life."

"What would I want with video games?" Kane asked, playing along with what he viewed as her outrageous scenario. "I don't even know how to play one."

It was Kelly's turn to stare. "You're kidding me, right?"

"I thought we already established that I never kid," Kane reminded her.

"I'll just get Valri to give you a crash course in gaming. She was a gamer for a while," Kelly told him, fairly confident that Kane didn't know. "She was pretty damn good at it, too. Won tournaments and everything—had my father pretty worried for a while," she confided.

"A gamer," he echoed. "I take it that's someone who plays games."

Kelly shook her head and grinned, doing her best not to laugh. "Can't put anything over on you, can I?" she asked, amusement sparkling in her eyes. And then she abruptly changed the subject as she remembered something. "Tell you what, since we're already here, why don't we go pay your uncle a visit, see how he's doing, before we report back to the precinct?"

"Sounds good," he replied.

For the second time in as many minutes, Kane felt a very strong urge just to pull her into an alcove, sweep her into his arms and kiss her. He realized that since he'd made love with her, no matter what they were doing, his thoughts kept coming back to Kelly. Back to wanting her.

And even more now.

His uncle was right. She *was* a keeper. He just had to be clever enough to figure out how to do that.

"We need to talk," he told her—then drew her into that alcove he'd just been fantasizing about. He wanted to talk to her away from the rest of the foot traffic. What he had to say was private.

"I always hated that line," she told him, doing her best to hide her uneasiness. "Can it wait? We just solved a string of home invasions and that means we get to write up the report," she reminded him with a touch of sarcasm. That was when she remembered their bargain, the one she'd made with him in order to get him to attend Andrew's brunch. "Tell you what. Since I am a woman of my word, I'll write up our report and you can go and do whatever it is you do after you solve a case."

She waited for Kane's response, assuming that he would take her up on it since *no one* liked to write reports.

His answer was not what she expected.

Rather than happily agree to let her do the work, or dutifully refuse to allow her to handle the burden alone, he said, "You're babbling."

Kelly did not respond well to what she took to be criticism. "I'm making perfect sense," she countered.

"You're babbling," Kane repeated quietly. His eyes took her prisoner. "Why?"

She wasn't about to allow him to interrogate her. "One person's babbling is another person's talking," she argued.

Kane went on as if she hadn't said anything. "Most people babble when they're nervous. What are you nervous about, Kelly?"

"Being accused of babbling," she answered defiantly.

Kane's eyes narrowed, effectively pinning her in place. He wasn't buying it.

"Talk," he ordered.

"I thought I was." Even so, she squirmed under his intense scrutiny. And then she gave up all pretense and just told it to him straight. "You had a strange look in your eyes and I— Well, I just didn't want to have to hear you say that you've decided to put in for another partner."

Where had that come from? He certainly hadn't given her any cause to think he was ending their association. If anything, he thought he'd done just the opposite.

"Why the hell would you think I was going to do that?" he asked.

"Because that's your style. You go through partners like a person with a cold goes through a box of tissues." She glanced away for a minute, gathering her courage to her. "And because of what happened between us," she added in all but a whisper.

God, but she had gotten her wires crossed this time. He was going to have to do something about improving communication between them, Kane thought.

His eyes captured hers. "Did it ever occur to you that it's *because* of what happened between us that I wouldn't want to change partners?"

"You wouldn't?" she questioned, allowing her uncertainty to surface.

"Let me see if I can make this clearer for you," he said, searching for the right words to get through to the woman who had suddenly come to mean so much to him. More than he would ever be able to convey. "You're like the refrain of a song that's stuck in my head, making me crazy, but I can't seem to unstick you."

She looked at Kane, trying to absorb what he was

actually telling her. And then she grinned. "I can make that work as a compliment," she finally said.

"It's not a compliment," he contradicted, being honest with her. "It's just the way things are. And I like the way things are," he told her before she could take what he was saying to her otherwise. "I like them *because* of you. Now *that's* a compliment," he concluded.

"So we're going to stay partners?" Kelly asked him as she drew a little closer to Kane. They were both ignoring the people who were moving around just outside the small alcove.

"Oh, I'd like us to stay a whole lot more than that," Kane admitted. "But partners will do for now."

The unfathomable look on his face was causing her heart to do some very strange, acrobatic things in her chest. But she was afraid to put a meaning to his words. There was a huge chance that she would be wrong. She needed to hear it from his lips, not just let her imagination take off.

"And later?" she asked in a hushed voice.

"Is later," Kane answered with a touch of whimsy as well as mystery.

Maybe it *was* going to turn out all right after all. "Do I get a hint?" she asked.

Kane pretended to consider her request for a moment. "Maybe one," he said just before he framed her face with his hands and kissed her very, very deeply.

Epilogue

He was late.

Of all the mornings she needed Kane to come in on time, he had to pick *this* one to be late.

They had been partners for six months now and she felt that was a cause for celebration. She had officially outlasted all the partners who had come before her—and who fled before they could reach this small milestone.

She wasn't going anywhere.

Kelly had all the necessary things for a small celebration laid out on the center table in the break room. In addition, she had talked Joe Spinelli, one of the other detectives, into playing lookout for her. He'd agreed to send Kane to the break room the second her partner came into work.

So where was he, she wondered impatiently.

For the third time she moved the cake she had brought in a fraction of an inch. Raspberry cheesecake. It was Kane's favorite.

Finding that out had been no easy feat, but then *easy* was not exactly a byword when it came to dealing with Kane.

Still, so far, so good. They'd made it work, she thought. Considering how fast he went through partners, she felt she had earned the right to be a little proud of herself.

Ordinarily, they came in together after spending the night at either her place or his. But last night, because she had this celebration in the works, she'd begged off, telling Kane she felt as if she was coming down with a bug and didn't want to risk getting him sick, as well.

He seemed to buy that—then surprised her later that evening by coming back armed with orange juice and chicken soup. If the man hadn't already won her heart, he would have gotten it right then and there.

After his obvious show of concern, it had been twice as hard to send him on his way, but she'd managed—and just barely had had enough time to make the cake.

She'd come in early to set up, then had spent the rest of the time worrying that Kane wouldn't come in for one reason or another.

What if he...?

She didn't get to finish her thought.

Kelly stiffened, listening intently. She recognized that voice. It belonged to Spinelli. The older detective was being deliberately loud so she could hear him.

His voice was growing closer.

Kelly struck the match she'd been holding in her hand for the past half hour. Once the flame appeared, she touched it to the lone candle that was positioned in the center of the cake. The candle was uncooperative. It took her two tries to light it.

Finally, at the last possible moment, the candle began to burn.

"Hey, Cavanaugh, Spinelli said you needed me to come into the break ro— What the hell is that?" Kane asked, coming to an abrupt halt several steps away from the table. He nodded at the cake with its lone burning candle.

"Well, and I'm only taking a wild guess here," she qualified whimsically, "but I'd say it's a cake with a candle in it."

"Any particular reason that there's a cake with a candle in it in the break room?" he asked her, displaying what he perceived to be infinite patience.

She felt a twinge of disappointment that Kane could be so oblivious to something that meant so much to her. But then, she already knew the man didn't exactly come with a marshmallow center.

"A very particular reason," she replied. When

Kane raised a quizzical eyebrow, obviously waiting for her to continue, Kelly sighed inwardly. He hadn't remembered. Okay, so it wasn't a big deal to him. But it was to her. A very big deal. "It's been six months."

"What's been six months?" he asked, appearing confused.

"Us." She pointed to him and then herself. "We've officially been partners for six months today. I've lasted longer than any one of your other partners," she added pointedly.

Kane looked properly surprised. "And you think that's worth celebrating?"

"Yes, I do," she answered stubbornly, challenging him to prove otherwise.

"Huh." With his hands firmly planted on either side of the cake, he leaned over and blew out the candle. Straightening again, he told her, "I would have thought that something bigger needed to be celebrated than just mere survival."

She put her hands on her hips, pretending to be annoyed. "Okay. What would *you* deem worth celebrating?" she asked.

"Oh, I don't know," Kane answered loftily. He paused, as if trying to come up with an answer in order to have something specific to point to. "How about this?"

"'This?'" she questioned when he didn't say anything further.

"This," he repeated, holding out his hand to her.

When she looked down at it he uncurled his fingers and exposed a small, perfect heart-shaped diamond mounted on a wishbone setting. The ring was in the palm of his hand.

Kelly stared at it, afraid to say anything, afraid to even venture assumption. Instead, she raised her eyes to his. "Kane?"

His immediate interpretation was that she wasn't happy. "You don't like it?"

Her mouth had gone suddenly very dry. For the first time in her life talking was a challenge. "Is this what it looks like?"

He wasn't quite sure what she meant by that. "What does it look like?" he asked her.

"An engagement ring," Kelly answered breathlessly.

"With a razor-sharp mind like that, it's easy to see why you outlasted all my other partners," he quipped. "Yes, it's an engagement ring."

Still, Kelly refused to allow herself to believe what she wanted so badly to believe.

"Whose?" she asked, her throat aching with what she assumed was the disappointment to come.

"Since it's too small for me, I'd say it was yours by default—if you want it. *Do* you want it?" he pressed, looking at her.

Kelly took possession of the ring, but still hadn't put it on. "Do you come with it?"

"I'm paying it off, so it looks like I have to," he answered flippantly. And then Kane put the banter aside. "I guess it's not official until I say the words." Not waiting for Kelly to say anything one way or the other, Kane said, "Kelly Cavanaugh, will you marry me?"

Kelly was struggling very hard not to cry. "Does this mean that you love me?"

Kane smiled then. It was a smile that easily reached up to his eyes.

"It's not always easy, but, yeah, I do. I love you, Kelly. Always," he told her in a voice hardly above a whisper.

She threw her arms around his neck then and cried, "It's about time because I love you so much it hurts," just before she kissed him, allowing Kane to become one with the heretofore missing part of his soul.

He'd finally found his partner.

* * * * *

MILLS & BOON®

The Rising Stars Collection!

1 BOOK FREE!

This fabulous four-book collection features 3-in-1 stories from some of our talented writers who are the stars of the future! Feel the temperature rise this summer with our ultra-sexy and powerful heroes. Don't miss this great offer—buy the collection today to get one book free!

Order yours at
www.millsandboon.co.uk/risingstars

**Don't miss Sarah Morgan's
next Puffin Island story**

*Some Kind
of Wonderful*

Brittany Forrest has stayed away from Puffin Island
since her relationship with Zach Flynn went bad.
They were married for ten days and only just
managed not to kill each other by the
end of the honeymoon.

But, when a broken arm means she must return,
Brittany moves back to her Puffin Island home.
Only to discover that Zac is there as well.

Will a summer together help two lovers reunite or
will their stormy relationship crash on to the
rocks of Puffin Island?

Some Kind of Wonderful
COMING JULY 2015
Pre-order your copy today

0315/MB507